Mountain Climbing In Sheridan Square

A Novel By

Stan Leventhal

BANNED BOOKS
Austin, Texas

A BANNED BOOK

FIRST EDITION

Copyright © 1988
By Stan Leventhal

Published in the United States of America
By Edward-William Publishing Company
Number 231, P.O. Box 33280, Austin, Texas 78764

ISBN 0-934411-08-5

This book is dedicated to my lover, Bob Locke.

—— Chapter One ——

On some August mornings, like this one, it's too hot to do anything that requires physical exertion. So I think and reflect. Try to sort everything out. And attempt to figure how I got from there to here. The past is neatly labeled and alphabetized on the shelves in my memory. The present is a blur of formless, oddly-colored shapes that have not yet found permanence in what will eventually be a completed pattern. And that is the one thing in which I maintain some faith; today's uncertainties will be tomorrow's finished episodes, ready for contemplation, thick with anecdotes.

Simply existing can seem to be overwhelming sometimes. I must sustain a career. Establish a new living situation. Maintain many relationships, both business and personal. All of this requires planning. There is always some new thing that must be thought out. A perfect example is the phone conversation with Jennifer, who called last night. We get along extremely well most of the time, our innermost parts harmonizing with no apparent effort. And on the few occasions when we've not been able to arrive at a point that is mutually agreeable, we push the topic aside and move on to something else.

When she called, she began by saying that there was nothing pressing that she wanted to talk about. She'd just wanted to chat. Inevitably, eventually, the subject that was bothering her rose to the surface sending tremors across the veneer that is usually so smooth. I asked about Magda, her two-year-old daughter and my surrogate niece.

"She's fine. Asleep and quiet. Guess what? She discovered the word 'not.' At dinner, she picked up her spoon and said, 'Not fork.' Then she pointed to her potato and said, 'Not bread, potato.' Later on she picked up a picture book and said, 'Not television,' then ran to the television and said, 'Not book.' What can I say, the kid's a genius."

"She's a *beautiful* genius. She'll make us all very proud of her. So, what's new," I asked, "heard any good ones lately?"

"None that spring immediately to mind," she said hazily, as though scanning her memory banks.

"How are rehearsals going?"

"Well, since you asked, I'm very angry. I had an argument with that asshole director because I improvised some body language to go with the monologue in the first act, and he said, 'A woman would never do that with her hands while talking about a deceased husband,' and I said, 'Well, this woman would,' meaning *me*. So he started yelling and then I started yelling and it turned into a huge mess. We both threatened to quit. It'll resolve itself by next rehearsal, but it was really upsetting because in the first place I don't think a man can tell me what a woman would do in *any* circumstances and in the second place I'm having trouble always being identified by my gender. Sure, I'm a woman. But that's not the beginning or the end. I'm a person first, a woman second, and then a lot of other things too."

We talked it over and she calmed down. I disagreed about her first point. I believe that there are those who are perceptive and observant enough to — with some accuracy — predict what a certain person would do in a particular situation. But on the second point, we were in complete agreement. We're people first. Gender representatives second. If at all.

When the conversation was over I thought about it in bed before falling asleep. And once the mist had evaporated from my mind this morning, the thought revealed itself again. From what perspective should I look at this problem of self-definition? And the idea suddenly struck me: from an Alien's, of course. Only a visitor from outer space could view me with complete objectivity, so that is how I must try to look at it.

First of all, I'm a man but have certain desires which have been designated as feminine. I was born in America and believe in Democracy, but our system of economics makes me uneasy. I was born into a Jewish family, but I believe in God about as much as I believe in Rumpelstiltskin. I am Caucasian, of European ancestry, but I love Oriental food, African music, and South American literature. And I'm gay, but unlike most of the gay men I know, I have very strong paternal feelings.

All of these assertions and denials, however, don't really capture my essence, I think. To those around me I'm a Jewish, white, American male. But according to the Aliens, I'm simply an Earthling. I like the sound of that. It classifies me with the other sentient beings on this planet and excludes me from non-Terran experience. It doesn't limit me to my birthright or separate me from anyone else whose forefathers and mothers were apes. The next time someone asks what I am I will not break it down into professional, ethnic, sexual, or religious categories.

"Well, basically, I'm an Earthling. If you have a couple of hours I can fill you in on the particulars. But for now, let's just say I'm from Earth. And you?"

*

I live in an apartment overlooking Sheridan Square, the noisiest intersection on the planet. Some people assume that it was my intention to live here because it's in the heart of

3

the gay and artistic ghettos of Greenwich Village. But the only reason I took this place was because it was the best deal I could find. My previous apartment was very small—about the size of a large closet—and when it was decided that Amos would move in with me I had to find something with more space. I looked at forty-six apartments in the Village and Chelsea. All were too small or too expensive. I finally wound up here, on the fourth floor of an old building. My windows face south and I have a grand view of the park below. The location is ideal for getting any place I have to get to in a hurry. But the confluence of many streets, the traffic and tourists, the bums that live in and around the park—all join together, creating a noise level that can be maddening. At first I was awakened by every screeching tire and screaming drunken tirade. Now an ambulance and a fire truck can both go by simultaneously, sirens cranked up to maximum, and I am completely oblivious.

Most of Manhattan is divided into a perfect grid. The streets run east and west, the avenues north and south. It's not very difficult to figure out where you're going once you've memorized the simple layout. But in the West Village this geometric regularity is, for the most part, abandoned. In addition to several streets that seem to pop out from nowhere, there are three important thoroughfares that cut diagonally across the usual perpendicular pattern. This can be very confusing at first. You find yourself walking down an ordinary street—lined with trees and staid brownstones huddled side by side—and you arrive at an intersection that is devoid of right angles. You must slow down and try to calculate which street most approximates the direction in which you want to go.

Sheridan Square lies at an intersection which is bisected by one of those diabolical diagonals. Like the hub of a giant wheel, the spokes point in all directions and it takes a few seconds for a newcomer to determine which street leads to the desired destination. Even then, you might not get it right the first few times. I know this to be true from my experience. And it is confirmed, almost every day, by some lost and bewildered tourist.

My apartment consists of a medium-sized living room — square shaped — with a tiny rectangular bedroom off to one side. The bathroom is adjacent to the kitchenette. Along the far wall of the living room are two French windows that open out onto Sheridan Square. Of the two walls alongside, one is buttressed by a bed that I use as a couch. Opposite is the television, stereo, and floor-to-ceiling industrial shelving packed with books and records. A few posters and art reproductions adorn the walls and the parquet floor could use a waxing that I haven't had time for. This is the room where I broke up with Amos and first made love to Mike. Where I chat on the phone with Jennifer, talk about art and politics with Donald, write my stories and reviews. Next to the French windows are a swivel chair and the bridge table that supports my typewriter, dictionaries, and telephone.

When I wake up in the morning, I usually fix myself a cup of coffee which I drink while looking out the window. In winter, the trees are naked and vulnerable; as bleak and austere as the surface of the moon. In summer, the mass of green leaves right outside the window gives the impression that I'm living in a treehouse. But the heat of July and August makes any odors inescapable. So when the windows are open, the stench — rising from the uncollected garbage and ubiquitous winos — flies into the apartment and slaps my olfactories, wrenching me from any fantasies about a treehouse paradise.

I'm caught right now in the transition of moving out the debris of an old love affair and getting ready for a new person to move in and share this space. I hope I don't repeat all of my previous mistakes.

When Amos moved out he left a lot of reminders behind and I confess I was too lazy to get rid of all of them. Now that Mike is to move in, I have no choice but to make room. For the past several days I have been gathering Amos' castoffs and throwing them away. The only thing I'm going to save is a poster he gave me which celebrates the 1979 Mardi Gras in New Orleans. It's a print of a sexy man wearing nothing but a jewel-encrusted loincloth and an enormous headdress bedecked with peacock feathers. It's the only thing of Amos' that I consider worth keeping. I don't think Mike will mind having it around. And if he does, he'll have to get used to it. There are many things that both of us will have to put up with, but that's okay. I believe that certain adjustments will have to be made. If we are both capable of some flexibility and are willing to talk things over, everything will work out fine.

*

When I look back on my relationship with Amos, the memories are like stills from a television cartoon. There's Wily E. Coyote going over the edge of the cliff. He's poised motionless in midair and doesn't plummet until he notices there is nothing between himself and the ground except fifty feet of empty space. I see Amos sitting at a table. A cigarette in one hand, a cup of coffee halfway between the saucer and his mouth. I recall our meals together and the stills become animated, as though following a predetermined script. Smoke issues from his nostrils as the cup reaches his lips. He chugs the contents. The scene plays out until the inevitable argument in which one of us leaves, slamming the door. I begin to wonder how I ever got involved with him in the first place.

My affair with Amos began with an invitation that came from an acquaintance named Ed. His name could have been Edgar, Edwin, or Edward. I never knew for certain. Ed and I used to hang out with the same crowd but we were not what I would call close friends. We weren't enemies either, we just happened to know one another. It came as a surprise when he phoned one day and asked if I'd like to join him on a trip to New Orleans.

6

"Are you kidding? Are you serious? I'd love to go. I've always wanted to." Then reality shattered my enthusiasm. "But I don't think I can afford it."

"Don't worry about the money—I've got it all figured out. The fare is less than two hundred and whatever you can't scrape together I'll loan you. Once we're there, we'll stay with a friend of mine so it'll cost next to nothing."

How could I refuse? My income is such that I rarely get out of Manhattan. I felt I could really use a break. And I was still a musician at the time and wanted to hear the local music firsthand.

"New Orleans, here I come."

Ed chuckled. "I'll make all the arrangements. We can have dinner tomorrow night and discuss the details. Later."

Elation filled my soul. I pulled out a reissue of 1927 recordings by King Oliver's Creole Jazz Band (featuring the young Louis Armstrong on trumpet) and lit a joint. The music and smoke lifted me even higher. It was with a renewed sense of purpose that I boarded the plane with Ed about three weeks later.

It was not until we arrived that I realized why Ed had wanted a traveling companion. The friend who was to be our host proved to be a very fat, effeminate man named Preston. He had tried to score with Ed while on vacation in New York. Ed, a bit vain and never at a loss for sex partners, had turned him down, but accepted his card and the offer to be his guest should he ever be in New Orleans. My function was like that of a shill; without ever saying it, Ed implied that we were lovers and that he was, therefore, unavailable as a repository for Preston's lust. I played along because I was equally unwilling to get involved with Preston, who made it very clear that either or both of us were welcome in his bed any time. His bulk and manner were so unappetizing, it was easy for me to act like I was in love with Ed.

This did not bother me too much because the ruse was necessary only when we were at Preston's house. Every evening the three of us went to the French Quarter together. We'd have a drink at a place called Fat Charley's. When the drag show started, Ed and I would leave under the pretext of seeing the city by night. Actually, we'd separate and cruise. New faces in town, we managed to score with a different local beauty (most of whom were not natives, but came from everywhere between Arkansas and Florida) every night. We'd meet at the Cafe Du Monde in the mornings to nibble beignets (semi-sweet pastries), sip chicory-flavored coffee, and compare notes about our conquests. I don't think we fooled Preston for a moment, but he was too polite to show any displeasure.

During the day we wandered the streets of the French Quarter while Preston was at work. We planned our own private, spontaneous sight-seeing tours. We visited a Dixieland bar and heard "Muskrat Ramble" at one o'clock in the afternoon, guzzling some horrible concoction called a "Hurricane." The Museum of Voodoo attracted our attention and we giggled and chortled over shrunken heads, fetishes, and talismans safely enshrined in glass cases. But the best attraction of the city was the architecture, plants, and flowers. The buildings are French and Spanish colonial — with ornate wrought-iron trellis work — painted in shades intended for the Mediterranean sun. The bright flowers and lush vines that scamper all over the buildings are tropical. This meeting of European design and Caribbean flora is what gives the French Quarter its unique atmosphere, probably the most exotic place in a country full of diverse styles and unusual hybrids.

We watched the artists painting and listened to the street musicians in Jackson Square and played country and western songs on the jukeboxes in the gay bars. In the evenings we'd be back at Preston's for dinner and depart for the Quarter to pursue sexy southern boys and men after clearing the table, doing the dishes, and leaving Preston at Fat Charley's.

On our last night in New Orleans I stood by myself in the Bourbon Pub, silently saying goodbye to the city I'd come to love. A bartender gestured at me and indicated that I should approach the bar. "What are you drinking?" he asked.

"Peppermint Schnapps," I held up the glass containing a drink I'd never had before which is something of a favorite among New Orleans' gay guys.

"That gentleman," he pointed to a cute guy who stood about ten feet down the bar, "would like to buy you another one."

I'd never been the recipient of a free drink from a stranger before and felt very flattered. I went over to thank him and introduce myself. He said his name was Amos.

*

I work in a box office, owned and run by a nonprofit, off-Broadway theater. I have been a taxi driver, factory worker, vacuum cleaner salesman, camp counselor, waiter, and clerk in a record store. I'm always leaping from one job to another, earning just enough to pay the bills, keeping as much time as is possible free so I can write. In the old days my "non-working" hours were spent composing. Unless you're a fixture on the bestseller lists or top-forty charts you must become a wage-slave in order to survive. I have learned to accept this.

There were two reasons why I decided to become a box office treasurer, aside from the fact that I needed a job and this one was available. For one thing, I lacked confidence and had to prove to myself that I could handle a job that required bookkeeping skills. Me, the worst student to ever make it through the American Educational System. The other reason was that the hours were flexible and I could create my own schedule each week. Since the pay is hourly — no salaries — I can work as many hours as is necessary to meet my expenses. The rest of my time is spent writing.

Box office work is unlike any other kind I've ever experienced. The main thing is that you are dealing with the public, something I thought I was used to, having been employed in a restaurant and a record store. But box offices are completely different. Have you ever wondered why the person selling you a movie ticket is surly? Why you were treated so rudely after standing in line for several hours to buy tickets to *Cats*? Why the treasurers in off-Broadway box offices can be so exasperating? I used to wonder. Now I know. It's because of the nasty attitude flung at you by total strangers. The stupid questions, snide remarks, and unreasonable demands. To say nothing of the rudeness that theater subscribers think is their right simply because they've purchased season tickets.

I recall one woman who almost made me quit. She, of course, wanted to sit front row center, which is where *everyone* wants to sit. But not everyone can. Two objects (or people) can not occupy the same space at the same time. And, not only could I not satisfy her requirements for seating, but the performance she wanted to attend was already sold out. She stood at the box office window looking like a clown — her complexion was too chalky-white, her cheeks overly rouged, and her lips too liberally painted, a bright scarlet.

"I'm sorry, Madam, but not only are all my front row seats gone, that performance is sold out."

"Sold out?"

"Yes."

"Does that mean there are no more tickets?"

"Yes."

"You mean, it's sold out."

"That's what I said."

"Not even two?"

"Not even one." I'm starting to get angry. There are mail orders I must process and phone calls I must deal with.

"What do I have to do to get tickets for that night?"

"There's nothing you can do."

"It's sold out?"

"Yes."

"Nothing's left?"

"That's what I said." I hate repeating myself. Why don't people *listen* to one another? Now I'm getting even angrier.

"But that's the only night we can go."

"I'm very sorry." I'm all sympathy.

"How come it sold out so fast?" She's getting frustrated. Thinks if she bothers me enough she'll get what she wants.

"Supply and demand."

"You mean to tell me you don't even have two tickets?" That does it.

"Madam, I can't sell you what I don't have," I say, angrily.

"You theater people are terrible! I'm going to write a letter. What's your name, young man?"

And so it goes. Jennifer takes great delight in making fun of these people and teases me sometimes when she calls me at home.

"Hello?" I say.

"I want sixteen tickets, front row center, for the Monday matinee," she wails in her best Brooklynese.

"I'm sorry, Madam," I say, playing along, "there are no matinees on Monday."

"But there's gotta be! I already arranged everything with the girls and that's the only time we can go," she whines.

"I'm very sorry."

"Young man," she snarls, "I'm going to write a letter to your supervisor. I want your name, social security number, and the size of your dick!"

I get a good laugh out of that and then she tells me why she really called.

*

I moved to Manhattan after completing four years of college in Boston, after completing eighteen years of childhood and adolescence on Long Island. When I was a teenager, I would have given anything to live in the city, but I am a child of the suburbs. From my vantage point in the land of country clubs and shopping malls, I yearned for the concrete canyons of concert halls, art galleries, old bookstores, and Bohemians. My neighborhood was ninety-five percent white and Jewish. I was eager to flee that set-up and meet different kinds of people.

When I moved to the West Village I began to hang out at a dance bar — now defunct — called the Chalice. It was there that I met a wide variety of people and soon figured out that the gay community cuts across every barrier that's ever been erected to separate people. Most people seem to gravitate toward situations where they come into contact with those who share their religious beliefs, country of origin, political persuasion, and tax bracket. I quickly learned that in the course of an evening at a gay bar, a poor artistic type like myself could meet wealthy businessmen, college jocks, intellectual lesbians, Hispanic drag queens, radical journalists, conservative priests, and Indonesian busboys.

One night, after working up a sweat on the dance floor with a thirty-five-year-old Episcopalian accountant with a famous investment firm, I was summoned to the table of a svelte straight woman who traveled by subway from Queens every night to hold court at the Chalice. With lustrous eyes and beautiful ass-length hair, Frannie collected pretty gay boys who would faun and compliment her, laugh at her obscene jokes. In return, she would arrange what she called "delicious couplings." If she felt that the twenty-two-year-old medical student with blond hair was right for the twenty-eight-year-old junior executive with bodybuilder muscles, she'd suggest that they dance together and would slyly spread the word that if they weren't already having an affair, they should be.

I became a part of her circle and in this way I began to meet other gay guys. Like Ed, who invited me to go to New Orleans. Frannie fixed me up with several guys who were attractive but did not interest me, until one night when she suggested that I dance with a handsome young man — an art student — who had recently arrived from Connecticut.

Donald — with a boyish face, quick wit, and husky voice — and I had sex a few times but found greater thrills in discovering gay writers. He told me about Andre Gide. I told him about Walt Whitman. The sexual part of our relationship evaporated and we found that we were friends. Our time spent together revolved around gallery-hopping, literary chit-chat, and the occasional film or play. And when we found new boyfriends we were not jealous, but glad that our sexual lives became dependent upon others. In that way we could concentrate on learning the intricacies of establishing oneself in New York's artistic communities. He as a painter. Me as a musician.

Donald and I are no longer in touch with Frannie. She disappeared from the scene around the time we stopped going to the Chalice. I ran into her a couple of years later. She looked stunning. She'd gained a little weight in the right places and cut her hair at the shoulder. "I'm finally engaged," she said. I wondered if she used to hang around with gay guys because she didn't think she could snare herself a man and if her desertion of her pretty boys coincided with her finding a mate. But I didn't ask. I wished her well, thanked her for all the good times, and told her to stay in touch.

When I called Donald he said, "Well, she finally found a man."

"She deserves it," I said, "but the Chalice will never be the same."

"Some other lonely girl from Queens will probably take her place," said Donald. "After all, a gay bar without an elegant fag-hag is like sex without the orgasm."

—— Chapter Two ——

The civic organization that maintains Sheridan Square Park is in the process of renovating. Only the trees remain from the original incarnation. New bricks, benches, and gates are being installed by several teams of construction workers. I watch these men from my fourth floor window and wonder what they think of all the passersby. I try to avoid the temptation of presuming anything about strangers, but it's not easy. Construction workers are supposed to be uneducated, heterosexual, and conservative. But surely there must be at least one — somewhere — who is none of these, if for no other reason than to confound the simplicity. "The exception that proves the rule," as my friend Max would say.

But my construction workers — mine because I watch over them, lust after them, write about them — seem to fit the rule. They are completely oblivious to my attentions. To them I am simply another pedestrian. A white male who comes and goes, just another integer in the equation of souls who parade through Sheridan Square every day.

I wonder what these laborers think of the men who walk by arm in arm, the women who greet each other with hugs and kisses that are too passionate to be dismissed as sisterly affection. My workers do everything in such a way that I can't imagine them as anything other than straight. They ogle the pretty women and whistle at the ones who look easy. Their pants are too loose, their hair too unkempt, their stride too determined for anyone to mistake them for gay. But perhaps one of them is only playing the game. Successfully. The game that millions of gay workers play to avoid getting hassled by employers and coworkers.

I sip my coffee and see two men approach the park. One has his arm around the other's waist. The other cups his lover's tightly-jeaned buttocks with his hand. I look at the workers to see how they will react. They don't. No insults, no wrists going limp. Perhaps they've been working here so long the shock has worn off. Maybe they just don't think about these things. Something tells me it's what anyone would expect in the West Village of Manhattan, so what's the big deal? Maybe they're all gay and play the game like pros.

I watch all the people moving through the square and I admire the diversity. And the display of identity. While some people hide who they really are, others flaunt it with impunity. That one's straight. That one's Hispanic. There's an Oriental queen. Here comes a black lesbian.

To the Aliens though, we're all just human. Earthlings. They'd notice that some of us are heavier, some taller, that there are variations in skin tone, facial structure, hair — length, color, and texture. That all of us, whether we like it or not, are either male or female, in a purely biological sense (the protuberant breasts and bulging crotches are a certain giveaway). Basically, we're all the same. We eat, sleep, fuck, and shit. Therefore we are human, all bound to the same revolving, circling orb, third planet from the sun.

The Aliens look down on Sheridan Square and see all the silly humans wandering around. Ethnic background, sexual orientation, and yearly income mean nothing to them. We are a different race. Therefore we are all the same.

Someone told me that liquor is the biggest business in New Orleans and I'm inclined to believe it. Preston, for example, would always fix himself a cocktail before driving anywhere and sipped it while doing any traveling — to work, to the bars, to shop. He kept a fifth of bourbon on the floor beneath the driver's seat to replenish his drinks as the ice watered down the alcohol.

In the French Quarter the bars are open all night and stagger their closings for the cleanup hour so there is always some other place to go. Near the door of every drinking establishment is a stack of plastic cups, so should you decide to leave before finishing your drink, you simply pour the contents from your glass into the plastic cup and depart. It's legal to drink on the streets, except from glass containers. So if you want a cocktail and do not wish to hang out in a bar, you can order it to be mixed in a plastic cup to begin with and hit the streets as soon as it's paid for.

One guy I went home with one night kept a bottle of wine by his bed and belted a shot right before going to sleep and another as soon as he woke up. After three days in New Orleans I decided that it was a lovely place for vacationing, but living there would be out of the question. For me.

*

Last night, Mike and I had dinner with Jennifer and her new boyfriend, Russell Stone. "His real name is Steiner but he doesn't think the American public is ready for an openly Jewish rock star," she'd said when I first heard about him.

She looked exquisite as usual. Her auburn hair has grown out considerably this year and looks radiant cascading over her slender shoulders. While many women's faces always look the same, hers depends completely upon her hair. Pulled back and knotted up she's a French socialite. Curled and sprayed, she's a suburban housewife. Last night she looked like a gypsy.

Russell Stone is her latest conquest. Hers usually last as long as mine which is why we always have so much to talk about. I hadn't met him before, but she'd told me plenty on the phone. "He's as talented in the sack as he is on stage," she'd said. "With a sumptuous butt and a cock to match."

"Good thing he's straight. For you, I mean. When's the wedding?"

"Oh, he's not marriage material, but a good lay for now."

Mike and I met them at my favorite restaurant. A small place the tourists haven't discovered yet that serves the best beef stroganoff I've ever tasted. The walls are adorned with blowups of thirties and forties film actresses, the lights are kept dim and the place is never too packed or noisy. The four of us sat at a small table in the corner with Barbara Stanwyck staring down at us.

Jennifer was right about Russell's ass; firm and well-rounded. His black hair was fashionably layered, framing a friendly face with dark eyes. In a cotton print shirt with a repeating pattern of small foreign cars, tight turquoise corduroys with black belt and gray suede ankle boots, you couldn't miss him if you tried. The pin attached to his shirt pocket said "Rock Star" in gothic letters.

Introductions were made and I noticed a slight British inflection in Russell's speech. I asked if he was from England.

"I'm from upstate, actually. But I'm a real Anglophile, you know?"

Jennifer sipped her Compari and soda and said, "He's got every record ever put out by a British band."

"Not all of 'em," he corrected her, "but lots."

Mike, who is beginning to feel comfortable around Jennifer, hardly said anything all evening because he'd never met Russell before. When Russell asked him what he does for a living, he blushed and said, "I'm a designer." Russell waited for some exposition but Jennifer and I knew none would come so she jumped in with "He designs sets for all kinds of productions — theater, film, television. I saw his work for an off-Broadway production of *Pygmalion* last year and it was sensational." Mike blushed again and looked like he might spread his arms and take flight. The man who sometimes won't shut up when he's alone with me reverts to a state of acute silence with strangers. I knew that we could expect little more from him so I grabbed the reins of the conversation.

"Jennifer already told us how you two met, but I'd like to hear it from you."

Russell placed his Guinness on the table, ran his fingers through his hair and said, "Well, mate, I'm in a band called The Revulsionz and we were playing at the Hot Club. It must've been around two in the morning, right before the last set and I'm all soaked and sweaty. I went to the bar to get some ale and this adorable creature said, 'Hey, sexy rock star, can I buy you a drink?' So she came up to my place after the last show and we did lots of coke and then made love. *Ta-da.*"

Mike blushed and Jennifer chuckled.

"That's exactly what Jennifer said," I told him.

Russell buttered a bread stick and asked, "How did *you* meet Jennifer?"

"You mean, she hasn't told you?"

I looked at Jennifer and she shook her head.

"I just know you two have been friends for a long time."

"Someone put together this mosaic of a theater piece that was basically an antiwar statement with set pieces and music numbers interspersed. Jennifer played the part of a woman whose brother was killed in Viet Nam. I played lead guitar in the band. We were on the road for about two months and I was the only guy who didn't try to pick her up. So we became friends."

At about that time, our dinner arrived. Four steaming platters of the tastiest beef stroganoff this side of the Volga. The conversation simmered down to exclamations of how good the food was.

We decided to have dessert and coffee at my apartment (ours, actually, but Mike hasn't officially moved in yet). After thanking the waiter, we waved goodbye to Miss Stanwyck and wound our way through the maze of the West Village to Sheridan Square.

I brewed a pot of chicory-flavored coffee and rolled a joint. Russell arranged eight lines of coke on a mirror and we sat and listened to the most recent studio demo of The Revulsionz. It was a bit rough, not a final mix, but the dense textures and aggressive attack gave a good idea of what the group sounded like. Jennifer looked bored, as though she'd heard it too many times already. But Mike and I enjoyed it; different from what we were used to listening to and not as loud as a live performance.

*

Ticket Pandemonium, my present place of employment, started out as a bridge table and folding chair on Theater Row in mid-town Manhattan. An Urban Redevelopment Plan allocated some dilapidated warehouses to be sold, inexpensively, to several off-Broadway theater companies. Eight small auditoriums were built within the space of one block, and the table and chair were erected every afternoon so tickets could be purchased to the eight new theaters. Rather than each having to maintain a full-time box office staff, this single table and chair notion was very practical.

Some of the theaters began to thrive, attracting larger subscription audiences and praise from theater critics. Ticket Pandemonium was moved from the table on the corner to a trailer parked on an empty lot several yards away. A telephone system was purchased and accounts with credit card companies were established. Bulletproof windows, a safe, ticket racks, and a voice-activated microphone were installed and Ticket Pandemonium was granted a new status.

About one year prior to my starting to work there, a few of the original eight theaters closed down. The remaining ones bought up the other's shares and Ticket Pandemonium was set up to handle their tickets and to seek clients from the worlds of off-Broadway theater and dance as well. At any given time, the box office handles from fifteen to thirty-five different productions. The number depends on the time of year. End of summer and mid-winter the number drops. During spring and fall we must work like madmen to get all the processing done that the number of clients demands.

Like the squat trailers that one sees at construction sites, Ticket Pandemonium can accommodate four people comfortably. But not all that comfortably. The air conditioner can barely keep it cool enough during the summer for we poor treasurers to avoid wilting like lettuce in a wok. And the space heater has as much effect against the cold as a matchstick in a meat locker. But we strip ourselves down to tanktops and shorts, or bundle up with sweaters and leg warmers, as fits the occasion.

Most of my companions at the box office are congenial types. We must get along. Working so closely in such a tense atmosphere necessitates comradeship. Those that don't get along don't last. But in general the turnover is rapid, as most treasurers at Ticket Pandemonium are actors, dancers, or singers waiting for their next part.

I'm the exception.

There are two kinds of customers that we service: the nice ones and the unpleasant ones. The fact that we handle many shows makes it easy to separate them. The nice ones tell us the name of the play they want to see, the date they want to see it, and the number of tickets desired. They number one in about seventy-five.

The unpleasant ones look at us blankly and say, "Two," as if we were mind readers and knew which play and which performance. Or they say, "One for Saturday," as though the clothes their wearing would suggest which play and matinee or evening. But the most unpleasant of all are the ones who already have a reservation and simply spout their last name as if we were some kind of walking computers and the key word would magically make the right show, date, and time appear on a screen.

After dealing with this for hours at a stretch, you usually reach the boiling point. I remember the last time quite well. An older man with sagging jowls and disgustingly long nose hairs appeared at the window and said, "Cohen."

"Sir, I need to know the name of the show, date, and time."

He looked at me like I'd struck him. "I don't know, my wife made the reservation."

"Then I suggest you talk to your wife, find out the necessary information and get back to me."

"Can't you just look it up?"

"Sir, I'm handling seventeen shows and god only knows how many Cohens have made reservations. I wouldn't know where to start. Do you know what the play's about?"

"No."

"I'm sorry."

"There's nothing you can do?"

"Not unless you give me more information."

"You don't have to be so rude," he snapped.

Me? Rude? "Sir, I've not yet begun to be rude," I said firmly.

"You seem pretty rude to me."

"You seem pretty stupid to me," I said, but pulled away from the mouthpiece so he couldn't hear me.

That's why I still have the job.

*

My last night in New Orleans was exhilarating and frustrating. Part of me wanted to get back home, but the rest wanted to party all night in the city where parties are a way of life.

"The name's Amos," he said. He stood about five feet, seven inches, all lithe and wiry. With his high cheek bones, milky blue eyes, and unruly brown hair, he exhaled sensuality. "It's not every night that someone as handsome as you wanders into this dive."

I've never been good with compliments, so I ignored it. "What do you do for a living," I asked.

"I'm a waiter right now at a wonderful place called Everything Goes. The atmosphere is very theatrical and I get to dress up in costume. All the waiters do. It's really fun. Last week I did Peter Pan and this week I'm Zorro. But I'm going to study restaurant management and leave waiting tables behind. You?"

"I'm on vacation — I live in New York — and . . ."

"I knew you didn't come from around here."

" — I'm basically a singer-songwriter but I'm working at an electronics factory to keep my head above water."

Just then Candi Staton's "Victim" ended and Manhattan Transfer's version of "Tuxedo Junction" swirled out of the speakers. Amos began to sway with the rhythm and snap his fingers.

"I love New York," he said. "I was there about a year ago. I adore Studio 54. Do you go there often?"

"I went once but didn't have such a great time. I think if I'd been with the right person it would've been better."

He smiled. A flashy display of perfect teeth. "Would you like to take a walk?"

I nodded. We poured our drinks into plastic cups and walked up Bourbon Street toward Toulouse.

"I live in a small apartment and I have a roommate," he said. "We can go there for a while. But he gets off work in about an hour so we should be gone by then."

The apartment was very small, just like he'd said. It was completely bare except for a large mattress on the floor. "We used to live in a large, nicely furnished place, but there was a really bad fire and it's unlivable right now, so we're staying here temporarily."

"You sleep together?" I glanced at the solitary mattress.

22

"That's right. But we're not lovers or anything. It's just until we can move back to our real place."

He lit a candle and turned out the light. After we undressed and stretched out, he rubbed my chest. I reciprocated. We kissed feverishly in a tight embrace. All too conscious of our time limit, we quickly brought each other to the edge and seemed to climax in midair. We were dressing when his roommate arrived.

We returned to the bar and talked while sipping Schnapps. When the bar closed at around six in the morning, we went around the corner to another that had just reopened. We joked and laughed until I glanced at the clock and realized I had to meet Ed and Preston to go to the airport. I gave Amos my address and phone number, but didn't really think I'd hear from him, or see him ever again.

*

Donald called this morning and said the date for his first one-man show has finally been set. I've seen his paintings in group shows and they always stand out, juxtaposed as they usually are with canvasses that are too drab or conventional.

Most of the guys I met through Frannie are now a part of my history. I got along well with them, but as time went by we seemed to grow in different directions. Unlike Donald, most of them are afraid to use their brains, and so, have little to offer once you get to know them. Should the discussion encompass the latest disco hit or Hollywood schlockfest, they always have an opinion. But bring up anything more substantial and they regard you as a leper.

Donald and I remain simpatico because we are still curious about the world and welcome the fact that there is still so much to learn. I teach him about music and he teaches me about painting. Not that I'm learning to paint, or he, play the piano. But he takes me to exhibits and explains the significance and context of the paintings, while I play records for him and explain the interrelationships between differing forms of music. And we still trade books and squeal with delight every time we discover another gay author.

When I first met Donald he was studying at the Studio School. I could see the origin of his developing style. Many of his canvasses are abstract, with oddly-shaped swatches of bold colors. The others are representational. His subject matter ranges from nature studies to depictions of urban scenes to studio-arranged still lifes. Among my favorites are a study of a brightly-hued bird in a dark green forest, a portrait of three men sitting on a park bench, and a homey realization of his studio with tubes of paint and brushes everywhere. But the best of all is a series that is based on sketches that he made in my apartment. My stereo, record, and book collection are part of the background and I derive much pleasure knowing that my apartment has been immortalized.

I can't wait for Donald's show. He deserves the exposure. And I want to see my apartment hanging on the wall of some tony art gallery.

*

It was a few days after New Year's Eve — I remember distinctly because it was one of the coldest days that winter — that I met Mike. At the Corral, a bar across Sheridan Square. I assumed it would be empty due to the sub-zero temperature and biting wind. It occurred to me also that a lot of people might have had too much to drink while welcoming the new year and would not be eager to become inebriated again so soon. As I expected there were few in attendance.

Going to the bar had become a part of my regular routine. After an eight hour shift in the cramped space of the box office and another three or four hours spent writing in my tiny apartment, any other four walls provided release and escape. And the Corral was so close I could get there quickly enough to avoid frostbite and hypothermia.

The guys who work at the bar are friendly, generous, and the jukebox is the best I've ever encountered. All kinds of music—representing the history of the large-holed 45 rpm single—the entire program changed a couple of times a week.

I zipped up my parka and literally ran to the bar, hoping to find love, or at least decent sex, but predisposed to the probability that I'd be the only customer. I paid for a tequila cocktail, played seven songs including the Everly Brothers and Talking Heads, then leaned against the ledge that runs around the perimeter of the room.

A few minutes later—I guess a couple of songs had come and gone—a cute guy with cobalt eyes and dark hair came in and ordered a drink. He leaned against the bar directly opposite from where I stood. We looked at each other and then quickly looked away, bar seductions being a type of game in which the rules must be strictly observed or loss is inevitable. If someone suspects that you are being too eager or too aloof, the spell is shattered and you have to start again from square one.

For the next half hour we looked each other over but our eyes did not meet. I replayed certain information on the video screen in my mind and weighed the facts.

Yes, the AIDS crisis was reaching the proportions of a holocaust. Yes, two of my best friends had died as a result in the three month period prior to that cold winter night. No, I hadn't had any affection or sex for approximately ten months. No, I didn't think I could survive for another three minutes without them. I'm not sure about women, sometimes they seem to do all right going without for a while; or maybe they just hide the pain better. But all of the men I know—regardless of sexual preference—go crazy after a few weeks of abstinence. I was in the thick of the danger zone and knew that something had to happen soon or I'd become the grouchiest, most cranky man in the city.

The blue-eyed, dark haired stranger moved to the cigarette machine, half the distance between his original position and where I stood. I gathered my courage, walked over, and introduced myself. He said his name was Mike. We shook hands.

"I hope you won't think I'm being too bold," I said, "but I never would have forgiven myself if I didn't come over to talk."

"If you hadn't, I'd have gotten around to it eventually."

He told me he designed sets for theater, films, and television. I told him that I write. His eyes said that he was willing to get to know me better.

"I hope you won't think I'm being too presumptuous," I said cautiously, "but I was wondering if you'd let me kiss you."

We kissed and all of my inhibitions disappeared. I invited him to spend the night at my apartment. He accepted. And also accepted the invitation to meet again the next night, when I asked him the following morning.

—— Chapter Three ——

My adolescence was somewhat abnormal compared to most of the other kids that lived in the town where I grew up. I sensed, at an early age, that there were things that I wanted to accomplish. My peers were content to exist. I couldn't wait to reach adulthood and do serious things, while they clung tenaciously to youth and avoided any kind of responsibility.

While the other boys were playing football or getting into trouble after school, while the girls were learning their cheerleading routines or swooning over their Paul McCartney posters, I was reading novels, studying music, and practicing scales on my guitar. I'd rush home from school and lock the door to my bedroom before Mom could complain that I should be out playing games with the other boys. First I'd pick up whatever book I was immersed in — back then it was mostly classics by English authors or modern science fiction — and spend about a half hour escaping in my mind from my small, suburban town. Guitar practice was next — another half hour of scales, riffs, and barre chords. Then it was stereo time.

AM radio was my initial exposure to music. But when I started learning guitar I was determined to investigate all of the instrument's possibilities. In this way I discovered that music is a universe. The first classical album I bought was by Segovia, the first jazz by Kenny Burrell, the first blues was B. B. King, and Doc Watson was my first folk artist. I began to grasp the vastness of the music spectrum and my weekly allowance became predestined to fill in the gaps: opera, flamenco, piano concerti, electronic, and ethnic music, madrigals, avant-garde stuff, and Broadway show tunes. It wasn't long before I had a large collection of albums that included at least a little bit of everything. I liked all of it but had a few decided preferences.

My first love was folk songs. Not the pop variety of Peter, Paul, and Mary or the Kingston Trio. But field recordings of genuine ethnic types who made music as a natural, integral part of their lives. A long way from the glitzy showbiz fluff that was so endearing to my parents. Wayne Newton did nothing for me. Ballad singers from the Ozarks, fiddlers from North Carolina, bluesmen from Mississippi, and Cajun accordion players from Louisiana held a far greater appeal. I began to read about these obscure musical genres and eventually became something of an amateur expert. I would write to prominent ethnomusicologists and to my amazement, they would respond — to a sixteen-year-old high school student. The most notable achievement of those years occurred when a distinguished academic, who'd obviously had a slight lapse of memory, wrote to ask if I knew the American title of an indigenous Scottish ballad. I did. We began to correspond and I felt so grownup I decided to become a folksinger. I'd dig up old songs or unusual variants and sing them to all who would listen. I polished up my guitar playing, built a fairly esoteric repertoire, and began performing. At age seventeen I sang regularly on the folk music radio program broadcast from the university situated in the next town. I thought I had it all figured out. I'd become an internationally known disseminator of folk songs and would eventually retire and write science fiction novels. But predicting the future is one of the many things for which I have absolutely no aptitude.

*

"Welcome home. Of course we all missed you very much. I want to know *everything*," cooed Jennifer. I could hear her inhaling smoke. Tobacco or marijuana? I wasn't sure.

"I don't know where to start. It was wonderful. I was able to relax completely and I partied all the time."

"What's the city like?"

"Magic. Like being in another country. The architecture, flowers, and vines, it's romantic, sensual —"

"Didja get laid?"

"Every night."

"Anyone special?"

"Well, yeah, sort of. The last night I met this wonderful guy and I think if I'd met him the first night, I wouldn't have spent time with anyone else."

"Slut."

"No, seriously, he was terrific. Not just a piece of meat. We talked all night. About books, music, theater."

"I'm jealous already. What's his name?"

"Amos."

"You're kidding."

"Nope."

"Sounds like the son of a preacher man."

"He just might be. I never asked."

"What'll your parents say when they find out he's not Jewish?"

"What'll they say when they find out he's not female. Oi!"

Jennifer laughed.

"There's a lot to be said for those southern boys," I resumed. "they talk so sweet and they're so polite."

"I once had this dude from Alabama and *he* wasn't so

29

sweet or polite." By the sound of the whooshing I knew she was smoking a joint.

"Did you have a good time with him?" I inquired.

"For days," she exhaled.

"That's all that counts."

"Right."

*

It seems to me that most people have one of two impressions of what Aliens might be like. That they are either cute, cuddly, and friendly, or sadistic, ugly, and out to get us. But I don't think it's quite as simple as that. Why must Aliens adhere to the good and evil dichotomy that falsely simplifies conflicts and so conveniently divides our planet? I have to allow for the fact that there may be forms of intelligent life that do not think like us or look even vaguely humanoid.

Imagine a creature that either looks like a stone naturally, or can assume the guise of a stone. A being that is clever enough to act like we think a stone should act, and therefore could avoid detection. We silly Earthlings would look at it and say, "That's a stone," never suspecting that it might be anything else. Because we think that living beings must be something like us, or recognizably alien, we overlook many other possibilities. I try to keep my mind open, prepared for the otherness of things.

In my mind, any Aliens which are smart enough to find us before we find them will regard us as highly amusing and worth observing, or completely insignificant and a waste of their time.

*

"Donald, it's me. I'm back."

"Hey, Mr. Jetset, how are you, how was the trip?"

"Fantastic. I've got lots to tell."

"I'll bet. Listen, I gotta run. I'm late for an appointment. We'll have dinner and talk. But first I've got to tell you something."

"What?"

"I sold a painting."

I let it sink in. "You're kidding! That's great. You'll have to tell me all about it."

"Are you free Thursday night?"

"Yes."

"Mexican okay?"

"Yum. I can't wait."

"Great. Bye."

I killed some time reading a book, packed up my guitar, and was out the door. I made it to the studio about twenty minutes ahead of schedule.

I was working with a new group that had just congealed. A mixed batch of musicians who played in different styles, trying to create a new sound. But it wasn't working. The lead singer was too Vegas schmaltzy and incapable of any subtlety whatsoever. My folkie/country harmony did not blend. The drummer had only played hard rock and was having trouble with dynamics and jazz phrasing. The keyboard player was too much of an attention grabber and the saxist wasn't assertive enough. My rhythm guitar was completely lost in the resulting texture.

Nothing came of this awkward combination except that the drummer, the band member who always had the best smokin' dope, gave me the number of his connection. He scribbled seven digits and an address on a small piece of paper.

"Call this here number and don't be freaked when the guy says 'Charm School.' That's the right place. Just say Sammy gave you the number. Everything'll be cool, you know? Tell him you want to take a class in Etiquette."

Two nights later I dialed the number and listened to the phone ring twice.

"Charm School, may I help you?"

"Hello. I got this number from Sammy. I'd like to take a class in Etiquette."

"Is this evening good for you?"

"Yes."

"Say around ten o'clock?"

"That's fine."

"You know where we're located?"

"Yes."

"See you at ten."

The Charm School was conveniently situated a few blocks south of Sheridan Square, so it took me less than five minutes to walk there. I rang the bell and was buzzed in. At the top of the third landing a door opened and a very tall and thin black man, wearing an orange sarong, invited me in. He closed the door and held out his hand. "My name is Max. You play in Sammy's new band, right? He told me all about you. 'Cept he didn't mention you were cute. Lots of straight guys have that problem."

I laughed and followed him down the hall to a room lit with candles. Large posters of a gorgeous black bodybuilder hung on the walls and the scent of musk pervaded the air. Billie Holiday's "T'ain't Nobody's Business" was playing on the stereo. Max lowered the volume.

"Why don't you sit over here?" He pointed to a couch upholstered in off-white damask. I sat on the left, he on the right. A long coffee table with assorted drug paraphernalia stood before us. He placed a cigarette in an ebony holder and lit it with a disposable lighter. "Have you come for smoke or coke?"

"Smoke."

"Exotic or commercial?"

"The cheapest stuff you got."

He assumed a look of mock indignation. "Sugar, none of my stuff is cheap. Some is just less exotic."

"Your least exotic then."

"How much?"

"An ounce."

Rising, he sashayed out of the room, returning in mere seconds with an enormous zip-lock baggie packed with grass. He measured out an ounce on a triple-beam balance that occupied the space on the coffee table between the coke mirror and the hookah.

"Since this is your first time here I insist you smoke a joint now, so you'll know what you're getting."

He rolled a thick joint and passed it to me. "Fine and Mellow" emerged from the stereo. I lit it, inhaled deeply, and passed it back. He accepted it, drew heavily, and returned it to me.

"Now, sugar, I'm sure you're dying to ask me all kinds of questions," Max raised his eyebrows and gestured with his head to the bodybuilder posters, "but I'll answer 'em before you ask 'em. You smoke, I'll talk."

I nodded.

"My given name is Maxwell but when I perform I'm Maxine, The Black Drag Queen. This little number I'm wearing is just something I threw on 'cause I was expecting company — you. I used to wear it back when I did Dorothy Lamour. But I don't do white folks no more. I do Tina Turner, Gladys Knight, Patti LaBelle, and Aretha, of course."

"No Diana Ross?" I asked, truly amazed.

"Don't be silly, child, she's been done to death. Besides, she never should have left the Supremes."

I chuckled.

"You're probably wondering about the photos of that very handsome man on the wall," he gestured with the cigarette holder, "that's Jack. He's a professional bodybuilder and he used to be my lover before he lost his mind and fell in love with someone else." Max made small circles in the air and pointed to his head.

I offered him the joint but he waved it away. "I supply good dope to half the creative people in this city. I make a good living at it so I can perform when and where I please without commercializing my act." He sighed, drew his long legs up and sat crosslegged on the couch. "Sammy told me you're the best Jewish country singer he's ever heard."

"I'm the *only* Jewish country singer he's ever heard."

"Let me tell you something. I'm thinking of working a little country music into my act so if you know of any good songs, you tell me about them. I'm always looking for new material and Sammy says you know your stuff."

By that time I was pretty dazed. Max kept chatting but I really couldn't pay attention. I said that I had to leave and asked him how much I owed. I placed the money on the table and he handed me the rolled-up, sandwich-sized baggie. He led me to the door and said, "You can call up any time you want."

"Thanks, I will."

"And keep me in mind next time you hear a good song."

"Okay."

"Bye, sugar."

*

I sometimes wonder if other people think about some of the things that I do. And wonder if *they* wonder what others are thinking. I think about evolution and history. Like the amount of time, experience, and technological advancement that it took to bring mankind to the stage where we could manufacture something as common as a pencil. Then I try to imagine how much mental and physical sweat went into the creation of a nuclear reactor. It's very humbling. I suppose it's good to be awed back into place sometimes.

But occasionally I think that the most awesome thing of all is the amount of suffering that we either succumb to or endure. And I wonder if there is some cosmic pendulum that ultimately balances out the pain and joy. Do some people suffer more than others? Do the ones whose suffering is greater — if there is a disparity — also experience more moments of ecstasy? These questions haunt me, yet they appear to be impossible to answer.

On the scale of human misery — considering abused children and populations destroyed — my problems are nothing. Still, only in my most rational moments can I realize this. Engulfed by complications or pain, I become irrational and find myself a prisoner of self-pity.

And then I hear about a father who puts his cigarettes out on the body of his sixteen-month-old child. Or that twenty-five thousand people died in Colombia when a volcano erupted. And I wince to think that I should ever have anything to complain about.

*

Donald and I met for dinner at Casa Paco, a quaint little place that no longer exists. It's been replaced by a pharmacy. But I fondly recall the adobe walls with bullfighting posters and the moon cacti beside the candle on every table. We ordered frozen margaritas with salt.

"Listen, before I tell you about New Orleans, or you tell me about selling your first painting, I've got some fast-breaking news."

He dipped a tortilla chip in the jalapeño sauce. "Shoot."

"Well, the last night of my vacation I met this wonderful guy."

"So what else is new?"

"— and I thought I'd never see him again. But I got a telegram from him two days ago that said that he had to talk to me and that he'd call last night at midnight — which he did — and we talked for hours and finally decided that we had to see each other again so he's going to come for a visit next month."

Donald dunked another tortilla chip just as the margaritas arrived. "Long distance love," he sighed, "how utterly romantic."

"I'm so excited I could scream."

"Do me a favor and control yourself."

I sipped my cocktail. "So, big-shot artiste, how did you come to sell a painting? You haven't even shown any yet."

Donald gave me that look of his which means that he's straining to recall exactly how something happened. "While you were away I had some slides made of a few of my smaller things and I picked them up on my way to work. Some guy comes in to have some paintings framed and he started to flirt and ask me questions. When I told him I'm a painter he said he'd like to see my work sometime. So enterprising me said, 'I happen to have some slides right here.' He looked at them and bought one on the spot."

"Which one?"

"A landscape I did in Austria last summer. The one of the mountains and hayricks."

I raised my glass and we toasted. "Congratulations. Next thing you know you'll be on the cover of *Artnews*."

"Congratulations to you. Next thing you know we'll be hearing wedding bells."

"I'm the one whose jealous. I could sure use a career boost," I confessed.

"I could use a good shot of love," he admitted.

I told him all about the trip to New Orleans and the first thing he said was, "So you and Ed are getting chummy, eh?"

"Funny 'bout that. He never called me before in my life. We've been back for a week and he hasn't called. When I called him to thank him for bringing me along, he said he was too busy to talk."

"That Ed," said Donald, "he's a strange one."

"Agreed."

Just then sizzling platters of burritos, enchiladas, refried beans, and rice were placed before us. We ate enthusiastically. Ordered more margaritas. The waiters shifted into second gear as the place began to fill up with customers. Or maybe we were slowing down from all of the tequila. But we stuffed ourselves, drank a lot, and could barely move when it was time to leave.

*

New York City is in a constant state of metamorphosis. Turn a corner and your favorite bookstore has become a high-fashion boutique. Call your favorite restaurant to make a reservation and an electronic voice informs you that the number has been disconnected. Small, older buildings are demolished and post-modernist skyscrapers replace them, seemingly overnight.

When I woke up this morning there was a new tune leaping over my windowsills. It sounded like the highly rhythmic, strictly atonal song of dueling jackhammers. I sprang from my bed and ran to the window. Below, the street was torn up and huge sections of water pipes were scattered about. Several men in flannel shirts and greasy jeans were milling around drinking coffee from styrofoam cups, supervising two other guys who vibrated with the noisy pavement demolishers.

It's cooler now that September has arrived. Last night, for the first time since May, Mike and I slept beneath a blanket. He's off at work already, leaving me to straighten up. But I don't mind because I don't have to work at the box office today.

Last night we talked and finally set a date for him to move in. We figured two months is more than enough time for his roommate to find a replacement.

I'm still moving things around, trying to create space for Mike's things. I've thrown out clothing that I kept but haven't worn since high school, books that I'll never read once and books that I'll never read again. The records, though, are a problem. I've got thousands and new review copies arrive every day. What I should do is collect all the wretched ones I'll never listen to again and sell them for fifty cents a piece at the secondhand record store. But that would require time and energy, the two things I never have enough of. I'll probably just leave a stack of albums on the sidewalk for the first lucky passerby to peruse and select.

On my last day off, I was sorting through my underwear to see what should get dumped and came across one of Amos' jockstraps. I thought everything that could possibly remind me of him—except for the Mardi Gras poster—was long gone. I keep wondering if anything else will turn up.

Everybody's always talking about the attraction of people they see and say "He's not my type," or "She's my type, all right." And I've come to realize that I don't have a type. Not when I compare Mike and Amos.

Regarding their respective physical appearances, Mike has all the right meat in all the right places while Amos is a study in anorexia. They both have beautiful eyes, but Mike's radiate intelligence, a big difference from the blank look of Amos'.

In the area of personality they are extreme opposites as well. Amos will say or do anything to get whatever he wants and can be frivolous to the point of exasperation. Mike is so honest it's scary sometimes, and though he's as capable of joking around as anyone, he takes things very seriously. I suppose that's why he's doing so well career-wise.

I'm pretty serious about my career too. But there comes a time when you've done everything that can be done for the moment and you simply must wait for someone else to do their job before you can proceed with yours.

When my music career was winding down I began to spend more time writing. I decided to try and write some short stories and have completed about twenty to date. I submitted fifteen of the best ones to a small press publisher and waited six months. Finally—in desperation—I called and asked what was the status of my manuscript.

"It's only been six months," he said.

"Four months too long, as far as I'm concerned."

"These things take time. Some manuscripts sit around for years between completion and publication. I'll get to yours as soon as I can."

I'm not a patient person to begin with. And I need something to show for all the work I've been doing. I never cut that album that I always dreamed of recording, and for the past three years have had to turn down a lot of invitations because I had to work on a story. A book of short stories with my name on it would be substantial accomplishment. It would be nice to have a tactile object that I could place in someone's hands and say, "Here, this is what I've been working on for the past three years. Remember that party I couldn't make it to? Check out the third story. I was typing the final draft."

—— Chapter Four ——

Lately it's impossible to get through a week without a major disaster occurring somewhere. If it's not a family of civilians killed in Belfast, it's a bloody coup in Nicaragua. If a psychotic isn't terrorizing women in Newark, you can be sure there's a tense hostage situation in Lebanon. What's that? Eighty black people were murdered by the African militia? Four hundred went down in a jet off the coast of Japan? Someone was pushed off a subway platform, right into the path of an oncoming train? A sniper killed a dozen innocents at a suburban McDonald's? What about the nuclear meltdown in Russia?

The atrocities mount up and it's hard to feel anything anymore. Unless a tragedy occurs that affects someone you know and love. In the past eight months, four of my best friends died. Of AIDS. Frank, a carpenter and poet; Jonathan, an accountant with one of the theaters I work for; Sergei, an internationally acclaimed concert pianist; Raul, an exceptional writer of fiction and essays. But I'm finding it harder and harder to cry. Anger is replacing sadness.

The news about AIDS is grim. The number of reported cases is still increasing. I try not to think about it, but it's unavoidable. It hurts to know that so many fewer people died of toxic shock syndrome and Legionnaires disease when the government stepped in and made a real commitment to research the problem and find a solution.

AIDS is not a "gay disease," although it's been called that, and even if it were, gay people pay taxes too. The really depressing part, though, is that straight society perceives this as a "gay problem." But *they* are very much a part of a potentially larger problem. If the current situation is not dealt with swiftly and effectively, a much more tragic end will result. It is ironic that the people who deny proper help to afflicted gays are endangering their own health. It would be sad to look back and see that large numbers of straight people died because they refused to act upon a course that would save the people they so violently hate.

Homophobia can be hazardous to your health.

*

Amos arrived in New York about the middle of October. When I met him at the airport he looked so adorable in his tight jeans and red-hooded sweatshirt I lost all my reserve, kissed and embraced him. A straight guy — I presume — who was strolling by shouted, "FAGGOTS!" I started to move toward him. "BIMBO," I yelled, ready to break his face. Amos grabbed my arm. "Control yourself," he whispered.

We collected his suitcases and took a taxi to Manhattan.

The first thing we did, upon entering my apartment, was leap onto the bed and get naked. We made love like sexually-deprived starvelings trying to make up for the quickie we'd had to settle for at Amos' temporary apartment in the French Quarter.

What followed was a week and a half of whirlwind social activity. Each night we had dinner at a different restaurant, several times with friends of mine whom I wanted Amos to meet. By midnight we'd be at a festive bar or disco. During the days I had to go to work but I called in sick a few times so we'd have more time.

We rode to the top of the World Trade Center and looked out over the Greater Metropolitan Enclave. Sailed to Staten Island and back on the windswept ferry and fed the pigeons. Saw *Sweeney Todd* on Broadway and the original film version of *Show Boat* at a revival house.

One night we had dinner with Donald. It was crucial that my best friend and new boyfriend enjoy each others' company. I was nervous. The three of us sat at a small table in a large Chinese restaurant. Somewhere in Soho. It was jam-packed with boisterous people, sitting at closely-situated tables. The noise level was almost overwhelming. The enormous, high-ceilinged building looked like a renovated airplane hangar. Sounds were naturally amplified and traveled indiscriminately. None of the waiters or waitresses looked Asian.

"I'm glad you're finally here," said Donald, "I've been hearing so much about you I feel like I know you already."

"What?" said Amos.

Donald repeated himself.

"The last time I came to New York I stayed with my brother and sister-in-law. This is more fun." Amos patted my hand.

Donald chuckled. "Discovering that Manhattan is the world's biggest playground can be a scream. Living here is not so easy."

Amos looked at me and said, "I'd love to live here. I've had enough of New Orleans. Too many people go there and never make anything of themselves."

"Where are you from originally?" queried Donald.

"Augusta, Georgia."

"What made you move to New Orleans?"

"Every queen that grows up in the south wants to go there. Like Mecca. The ones that aren't born there wind up there eventually. It's *tres* gay."

Donald laughed.

Amos smiled.

I relaxed.

The food tasted like spiced plastic and our waiter was abrupt and surly. Amos seemed to enjoy the place but Donald and I swore we'd never return.

After we left, Donald said goodnight. Amos and I went to an after-hours bar and drank bourbon until five o'clock in the morning.

The highlight of our week and a half together occurred at Studio 54, still at it's height of prestige as the world's most exclusive, celebrity-filled discotheque. I wangled some invitations to a promo party for the signing of a new punk group.

When we arrived at the door, Amos was impressed because we passed by the crowds and entered like big shots. The dance floor was packed with New York's trendiest and the party vibrations could simply be plucked from the air.

The music was fine and we both got a big kick out of watching the styrofoam moon snorting fake cocaine. We arrived back at the apartment at about four in the morning dizzy from the excitement, sweating from the dance marathon, certain that we were falling in love.

*

Jennifer left a message on my answering machine last night. I returned her call this morning.

"Jen, it's me. What's up?"

"I got a callback for a soap I auditioned for last week. Russell has a rehearsal and my Mom's out of town. If you want, I'll bring Magda over to your place or you can come here. Just as long as I can be free from three to five."

"No problem. Where do you have to be?"

"Ninth and forty-second."

"I'll come up. I should be there by two."

"You're an angel. Magda couldn't ask for a better fairy godfather."

"Watch it, breeder. Who you callin' a fairy?"

43

"You. You're the best fairy a woman could ever want."

"I think there's a compliment in there somewhere, but I don't have the patience to go looking."

"There is, silly."

"See you tomorrow."

*

Sometimes people can be so exasperating that I find myself silently cursing everything, everyone, the planet Earth and outer space. I'll be standing in line, for example, at the supermarket. There are about five people ahead of me and I'm running late for work. Just as I'm about to relax because it looks like I might make it in time, someone in front of me gets unreasonable with the poor soul at the cash register.

"Last week this tuna was 89 cents, now it's 93 cents, what goes on?"

"It's called inflation."

"How am I supposed to live?"

"That's not my problem. I don't raise the prices. I just take the money and bag the groceries."

"But I'm on a budget."

"There are people waiting behind you."

"I don't care. I don't think I can afford to shop here anymore."

Good, I say to myself, go somewhere else.

The customer pulls out some empty soda cans to be recycled.

"You're in the wrong line for refunds," says the cashier.

"What difference does it make which line?"

"We have rules."

Fuck the rules. I'm late for work. I decide to intervene. "Look, I'll buy you a can of tuna and I'll give you a quarter for the cans, all right?"

"Mind your own business."

I leave my grocery-laden cart right where it is and dash off to work. That night I make a meal of stale crackers and blueberry preserves.

Maybe the Aliens are already here — disguised as humans — and so poorly have they done their homework, they tend to mess everything up. Or maybe something in our atmosphere causes their brains to disintegrate and their scientists have failed to uncover this problem. If this fact were brought to light I would not be at all surprised.

*

It was about 11:30 p.m. at a darkly-lit rock club, Lizard's Lounge, that we first heard The Revulsionz live. A dance floor, about the size of a billboard laid flat, separated the stage from the tables. And waitresses in hot pants or miniskirts served watered-down drinks to the customers who'd already paid a ten dollar cover charge for the privilege.

A tape of new bands with names like "Rathole Warrior" and "Childhood Pox" issued from the sound system. Girls and boys with chartreuse or magenta Mohawk cuts and safety pin earrings sang along. They knew every unintelligible word and inflection. A genuine 1980s hootenanny.

Our table — dead center, right at the edge of the dance floor — comfortably sat two, but Jennifer, Mike, Donald, and myself crowded together, our knees intertwined. Our waitress, bleached hair in a bouffant, metallic halter top, white vinyl miniskirt, and scruffy go-go boots, looked like she'd just stepped off a movie screen featuring *Lesley Gore Meets The Martians.*

"What'll it be?"

Jennifer, who'd spent too many nights in too many dingy clubs waiting for Russell, was bored. "Oh, make it a sea breeze, haven't had one in a long time."

Donald, who rarely goes to hear live music was all excitement. "Tequila, straight with salt and lime," he said, rubbing his hands together in anticipation of a special treat.

Mike, who prefers the Vienna Philharmonic to the Rolling Stones and had never — I believe — been in such a seedy spot, asked for "A vodka tonic, not too strong, please," in a

45

supplicating voice that betrayed his discomfort. I patted his knee (I hoped it was *his* knee) and he smiled as if to say, "It'll be okay."

I, who was used to being on or backstage at such places, was fascinated by the crowd and the bits of overheard conversation that penetrated the din, decided on Jack Daniels with ice.

The waitress tucked her pad and pen in the waistband of her skirt and moved through the crowd like an expert. "Comin' through, comin' through," she warned.

I noticed that a kid at the next table had already passed out. Just then the house lights dimmed and the band took the stage. Russell, in white spandex from neck to ankles plugged in his guitar, tested the volume and stepped to the microphone. "ONE, TWO, THREE, *FOUR,*" he screamed and the band lurched into an upbeat paean to womanhood called "Girls Of The World," which as its title suggested, celebrated global feminine beauty. If I remember correctly, the chorus went:

> I love the girls of the world
> Yes I do, yes I do
> I love the girls of the world
> And they love me too
> Yes they do
> Love me true

After the third song the waitress arrived with our drinks and knew exactly who got what. I sipped my bourbon and checked out the other band members as they dove into a "brand new tune" which I think was called "Frustration and Lust."

Standing next to Russell, singing harmony and playing bass, was a tall and skinny fellow in black leatherette with darkened eyes, rouged cheeks, and pink lips. The keyboard player, bald and emaciated, stood behind a wall of synthesizers and would press his groin against his instruments anytime he played a riff in the upper registers. The drummer looked vaguely familiar, but behind his trap set, with the lighting all diffused, all I could make out was a shredded T-shirt and biceps the size of cantaloupes.

The music was too dense and loud for me to notice anything special about any of the musician's ability, but I tapped my foot and strained to catch the garbled lyrics. Except for one number about being alone on a beach called (I think) "Solitude," they were all about girls and sex. I admit it was foolish of me to expect anything else.

Jennifer stared at Russell and watched our faces for signs of disapproval between songs. Donald smiled beatifically, kept rhythm with his head, and clapped enthusiastically after each number. Mike and I kept glancing at each other with looks that said, "This can't go on all night, it'll be over soon."

The kids around us were jumping up and down, yelling things like, "Rock on!" and "Whip it good!" When the set ended, the band came back for an encore and performed a revved-up, feedback-laden version of the Beatles' "Revolution." The kids went berserk. Mike sighed, leaned over and said, "My ears are ringing."

"I can't hear you," I said, "my ears are ringing."

He laughed sarcastically.

We paid our bill and Jennifer led us to the backstage area. Russell was soaking wet. After kissing Jennifer, he shook hands with Mike and I. We introduced him to Donald, who was beaming.

"Loved it. You guys were great. I think I noticed a strong influence from Chicago blues," he said.

"Chicago blues?" said Russell, searching his memory. "I don't think we've been influenced by Chicago at all. They're really a rather conservative band —"

"Not Chicago, the band," explained Donald, "you know, Chicago blues, like Muddy Waters."

"I think if we've been influenced by anything at all, it's Quaaludes and the Sex Pistols."

Just then the drummer emerged from the men's room and I could see his face clearly for the first time. Chico Valentin. We'd played together in several ill-fated combos. We embraced and he looked me up and down. "How're you doin' ol' buddy? I'd have thought you'd be a big star in Nashville by now."

"No, I quit the music business a few years ago. I'm a writer now."

Russell came over to where we stood. "You two know each other?"

"Best damned country drummer in New York," I said.

"Best damned gay country singer anywhere," said Chico, slapping my back.

"Does this guy still score three-four-five girls a night?" I gestured at Chico and looked at Russell.

"Like a maniac."

Chico laughed. "You're not going to believe this, but I'm getting married in two months."

"Never thought you'd go for it," I said.

I introduced him to Mike and Donald. Donald gushed about the power of the band's rhythm. Mike politely said hello.

Just before we left, Chico asked if I'd come to the wedding. "Are you still in Sheridan Square?"

"Yes."

"You'll get an invitation."

*

Mike says that if there's a God, it's probably a deranged bag lady who delights in mucking up everyone's lives and chortles heartily watching us try to surmount her various obstacles. I wish I could treat the matter so lightly.

I don't think there is a God—at least in the way that he, she, or it is described by devoutly religious types. They picture a being that consciously decides what will happen to whom, as though Earth were a huge chess board and all of us pawns—disposable and inconsequential. This is difficult for me to grasp. If there is a willful God, he, she, or it is surely the most cruel and merciless entity imaginable. Unworthy of worship.

The only forces that I concede to be more powerful than we humans are Mother Nature and Father Time. And I can't picture them sitting down to tea and arguing over who wins the lottery and who gets hit by a truck.

The problem, it seems to me, is that people can't separate fact from fiction. All of those ancient texts — from the Bible to the Koran — are works that grew from the imaginations of *people*. The events depicted therein have about as much to do with reality as *Star Wars*. The movie, not the intergalactic military strategy.

And when I really stop to think about it, organized religion has probably done more harm than good. Sure, missionaries brought aspirins and irrigation techniques to primitive peoples and the UJA plants trees in the desert. I have no problem with that. But what about all of the mistrust, superstition, violence, and hatred that have been perpetuated in the name of God. The fact is that anyone can twist any religious allegory into any shape they please and justify any action. They can also choose to glorify or ignore any religious parable to make any self-serving point. Religious fanatics point to Leviticus and condemn me for being gay. But the story of Ruth and Naomi's love rivals that of Gertrude Stein and Alice B. Toklas. And of course, religious folks never acknowledge that the Bible includes a torrid lesbian romance.

I think, ultimately, if every church, synagogue, and mosque disappeared tomorrow, the world would be a better place. Less beautiful perhaps. But infinitely more humane.

Whoever masters the secrets of the universe is God, if God there be. If the Aliens get here first, I guess they will have the right to call themselves God. If we get to their planet first, I guess we'll be stuck with the responsibility.

Heaven help us.

*

I don't know what the Chinese were calling it, but everyone I knew was calling 1969 the Year of the Pig. I had just arrived in Boston for my first year of college and the entire country was divided on the subject of Vietnam. I sided with the pacifists. Everyone else was considered a pig.

I was an unreconstructed folkie and was deemed quaint by all the Jimi Hendrix fans, Grateful Dead heads, and Pink Floyd freaks. There was no tangible hostility directed at me; I was simply thought terribly unhip. But I managed to find my niche. There were a couple of clubs on Charles Street that featured folksingers, so I resumed my performing career. I also met a guy who wanted to form a duo (Peter, Paul, & Mary without Mary), so I was kept pretty busy.

I had originally planned on pursuing a music career right after high school graduation, but the draft board stepped in. So, to avoid becoming a weapon in a conflict that disgusted me, I decided to go to college and get a student deferment. I was technically an English major and actually read all of the assigned books. But most of the classes didn't interest me. I was preoccupied with writing songs, developing my guitar technique, and exploring the limits of partying.

—— Chapter Five ——

A *Time For Peace* was the name of a theater collage that was first performed in New York City, and then toured the country. The Vietnam war was winding down and several writers and a director had put together a grouping of dramatic scenes interspersed with antiwar songs. Some wealthy liberals provided financial backing. I auditioned for the band and got the job. The money was pretty good and the production was in accordance with my pacifist stance.

Jennifer was the lead actress and brought the audience to tears at every performance. She shook her fist at the gods and the fates, imploring them to turn mankind away from death and destruction.

Most of the guys in the show were interested in Jennifer, but aside from a brief affairette with one of the actors, she spent most of her time with me. There were endless bus trips between cities and long nights at decaying hotels. Jennifer and I usually shared a room and talked day and night about every subject that came to mind.

When we came off the road we exchanged phone numbers. But neither of us took the time to call. She was busy looking for good parts and I plunged into the maelstrom of hiring musicians, organizing rehearsals, and cutting demo tapes.

The next time I saw Jennifer was at Max's.

I called to arrange an Etiquette class. He said I should come over right away — that class was already in session.

Entering the apartment, I expected that overpowering aroma of musk, but it had been displaced by the sweet scent of gardenias. They were everywhere, floating in small porcelain bowls of water. And sitting on Max's couch, her hair all spiky with an orange-streaked forelock, was Jennifer with a straw in her hand. And white powder on the tip of her nose. We kissed and I sat down beside her.

"I see you two already know each other so I'll dispense with the introductions," said Max, playing with a six-foot purple boa draped around his naked torso. Running shorts and sandals completed the ensemble. "Smoke or coke?"

"Smoke," I said, "but something exotic this time."

"Let me see what I've got." He trundled out of the room — still lit by candlepower — and I turned to Jennifer.

"So, how are you?"

She snorted a line of coke from Max's mirror and handed me the straw. "Try some of this."

The coke had not been tampered with and the back-of-the-throat-drip was not as bitter as I'd come to expect. A tape of Tammy Wynette played in the background and Max re-entered just as she started singing "Womanhood." He sat down beside me and said, "After your last class I went out and bought some tapes. Sugar, some of those country girls are all right!" He sang along with the tape and rolled a joint from each of three baggies. "Try this one first. It's Thai. Powerful good."

I inhaled and immediately felt myself to be free of gravity. I passed the joint to Jennifer. She took a hit and remarked, "Life is a banquet and most poor bastards are starving."

52

"You're still young, baby," said Max. "When you mature a bit you'll find that life is a toilet and most poor bastards are scrub brushes."

The three of us sat there for hours, smoking and snorting, listening to Max's newly acquired tapes of female country singers.

It was subsequent to that evening that Jennifer and I started getting together for dinner, and calling each other to discuss our triumphs and failures, our careers, and our sex lives.

*

For the first two weeks that I knew Mike all we did was have sex. We'd meet at the Corral at about 11:30 —almost every night—and after a drink or two, come over to my apartment. At first he was shy and reticent. But as he became more relaxed with me, I discovered that he had a wonderful sense of humor. Most of the guys I'd been with were very serious before, during, and after sex. But not Mike. I recall one particularly cosmic orgasm. I was sweating buckets and catching my breath when I gazed into his eyes and he quipped, "Was it something I said?" I laughed until it hurt and realized that he was someone I wanted to spend a lot of time with.

One night we were sharing a joint after sex and I figured it was time to see if our relationship was going to develop beyond the perimeter of my bed. Also, I wanted to find out his thoughts about the health crisis. I brushed his cheek and held his hand.

"There are a few things I've been wanting to discuss with you."

"Okay, Tiger Butch, I'm listening." His talent for spontaneous nicknames is only part of his charm.

"For one thing, I thought it would be nice if we spent some time together doing other things. Like having dinner, seeing movies. You know, stuff like that."

"That's fine with me. Why don't we have dinner tomorrow night?"

"Great, I know just the place, too." I felt like I'd just won the grand prize on a television game show. "And, I'd like to start meeting some of your friends and introduce you to some of mine."

"No problem," he smiled, his cobalt eyes glinting like pinwheels.

"Terrific."

"Is that all?"

"Well, no," I said, "this is the hard part."

"I'm listening."

"You, no doubt, have read all about AIDS?"

"Yes."

"I thought we should discuss it a little."

"Okay."

"Here I go." I was so nervous my stomach was quaking. "Prior to meeting you I was so freaked out about the whole thing, I didn't have sex for almost a year. And it started to drive me crazy. So I decided I'd rather live for another two years and have a normal sex life, than live for another fifty years and be miserable all the time."

He nodded. "I know what you mean."

I pressed on. "I was examined by my doctor a few weeks ago and as far as he could tell, I'm okay so far. But you and I have to face the fact that every time we have sex, we could be killing each other."

He breathed deeply and sighed. "I know. I've thought about it too. Let me say that as far as I know, I'm okay too. And I think if you and I can keep a regular thing going —and not fool around with anyone else—we can have sex and minimize the chances of contracting AIDS. Also, no more crabs, syf, amoebas, or any of that stuff."

"Sounds good to me," I said, greatly relieved.

He pulled me down and smothered me with kisses. The last thing I recall him saying before drifting off was, "Don't worry, Honey Bear. I'll take care of you if you'll take care of me."

*

Sometimes I wonder what keeps me going. And why the direction seems so inevitable. Nothing ever works out the way you want it to. Just enough so that things keep moving along until the arrival of the next crisis, or that rarity — good news.

I suppose it would have been much easier to follow the route that had been neatly prearranged. Marry a nice, Jewish girl. Have the 2.3 kids. Move to a split-level in the suburbs. Build a two-car garage. What could be simpler?

Obviously, I didn't choose an uphill road just to be willful and contrary. In fact, I'm not aware of choosing anything. My interests in music, literature, and men came to me as naturally as my green eyes, brown hair, and lanky frame.

Looking back — had I been given a choice — I think everything would be the same. I don't envy the guys I went to school with who are going through their second divorce, haven't read a book in twelve years, hate their work, and spend all their free time with their remote-control, color television sets.

Some people are content to watch their TVs. Some people are not content at all. Some people must climb mountains. And the first thing a mountaineer learns is that you must be as aware of what's behind you as you are of what's ahead. That is, if you want to complete the trip and make it safely back to level ground.

*

When Amos left New York and returned to New Orleans I was overwhelmed with contradictory feelings. I was still elated from our time spent together, but was saddened that it had been so brief.

We called each other several times a week. Wrote long, intimate letters, and told each other everything we did every single day.

A thought began to materialize in my brain and at first I was afraid to let myself succumb. But finally I quit trying to deny it and wrote a sprawling letter in which I eventually got to the nucleus, after circling it for several pages. I suggested that it might work out if we were to live together and then pointed out the assets and liabilities of his moving here and my moving there.

I concentrated mainly on our careers and pointed out that he could find restaurant work in New York with far more ease than I could establish myself on the music scene in New Orleans. He was used to jumping from one restaurant job to another while I had spent years trying to meet the right musicians, club owners, agents, and music publishers. Besides, if Amos was sincere about learning restaurant management, he could do it here and find many opportunities upon graduation. I boldly stated — while fearing the worst — that if I had to choose between a relationship and starting my career from scratch, I'd stay in New York and consider our affair as a finished chapter.

At the time I had no idea that he wanted to move here all along and was just waiting for me to bring it up. The last letter he ever wrote to me said that he'd arrive on May 1, two months from the day I received his message. I was as happy as I'd ever been and began the long search for a new apartment. A search that ultimately delivered me to the heart of Sheridan Square.

*

The Bearcats had started out as a garage band in a small town about an hour's drive from Boston. A power trio originally, they played songs by Cream, the James Gang, and Jimi Hendrix at high school dances. The bass player, Tom Mansfield, was enrolled in the same Jazz Composition class that I attended after leaving my English studies behind. We became friends.

After class he'd come over to my tiny space located in the Back Bay rooming house. We'd smoke joints and listen to all the jazz recordings we could find. Everything from Jelly Roll Morton to Cecil Taylor. He turned me on to lots of big bands: Stan Kenton, Count Basie, Thad Jones/Mel Lewis, and Maynard Ferguson. I was crazy about sax players and introduced him to John Coltrane, Wayne Shorter, Booker Ervin, Ornette Coleman, and Eric Dolphy.

One day Tom brought up the subject of the Bearcats. "I know the last thing you want to do with your life is play top-forty hits at high school dances, but dig, the money is incredible, you get practical performance experience, and the girls are just waiting to be picked, plucked, and fucked."

I ignored the part about the girls. I had just started going to the Boston gay bars and was beginning to feel comfortable with my identity as a gay man. I was not yet ready, though, to share that information with straight people.

"Sounds like a good idea," I said, "but you guys have a solid thing going without me."

"We could use another strong voice. And with you on guitar and keyboard, we'd be capable of doing stuff that gets beyond heavy metal."

"What do the other guys think?"

"They're all for it. Ever since I brought it up they've been pressing me to ask you."

"Let me think about it."

His points about the money and experience made a lot of sense. My parents had been supporting me through school and I was eager to be on my own. And what he said about performing experience really got to me. I hadn't been on a stage in almost a year. Not since the breakup of my folkie duo. Eventually I'd have to leave the cloistered comfort of music school and face the harsh realities of the music business. Why postpone the inevitable? Why not get a head start?

I informed Tom that I was interested and he suggested that I attend the next rehearsal. The drummer and lead guitarist were brothers. Friendly and slightly wiseass. Both were cute; handsome faces, good bodies. We played a few tunes by the Rolling Stones and the chemistry seemed to gel. I taught them a song I'd recently written and it sounded okay. They were thrilled that we'd be doing some "original material" (I gathered this would impress their girlfriends).

Our first few performances were at high schools. They went well and I was amazed by the money. Up until that time I'd earned about twenty-five dollars a night at a folk club. Suddenly I was earning two hundred for a couple of sets. I let my hair grow until it reached my ass.

Eventually we graduated to the college dance circuit where the money was even better. And soon after that we signed with an agent who got us jobs in bars and lounges. By that time we had a repertoire of about one hundred top-forty hits — from Chuck Berry to David Bowie — and we'd play two or three of the ten songs I'd written at each gig. We developed a small following and I started to notice the same faces in the crowd night after night.

Our big production number was "I'm Eighteen" by Alice Cooper. I'd put down my guitar, seize a long, yellow boa that Tom's sister had given me, and slink and slither about the stage — whipping my hair around, growling the lyrics. The audience always went wild and would request the song repeatedly. We would end up doing it three or four times a night and I'd get so hoarse I could barely speak.

The other Bearcats would screw different girls in the back of our van every night and I deflected their questions about my sex life by inventing an imaginary girlfriend who was waiting faithfully for me back in New York. In reality, I was hitting the bars in town and slowly learning about the gay subculture that I never dreamed existed, but apparently flourishes everywhere.

All this time, I was still taking my jazz classes, although Tom had dropped out. I wrote more songs and they kept getting better.

After about a year of this, I suggested that we start making demo tapes of my songs and try for a record deal and national exposure. I thought they'd welcome a career move, but I was wrong.

"Are you kidding?" said the drummer, "and fuck up a good thing? We've got all the gigs and chicks we need."

"Yeah," said the lead guitarist.

I decided that I was ready for bigger and better things. So I quit the Bearcats, dropped out of school at the end of the semester, and moved back to New York. I figured I'd be a rock star in a reasonable amount of time.

*

When I entered Jennifer's apartment — a small, one-bedroom in the West eighties — Magda was sleeping in her crib. Her mother was pacing around, pulling curlers from her hair with one hand, holding a script with the other.

"If you're not careful, Paul, I'll ruin you," she spat.

"I'm not Paul," I protested.

"Shh! I'm memorizing my lines."

I sat on the sofa and waited.

"I happen to know about everything that happened between you and Angela, so if you don't toe the mark, I'll tell her husband." She untangled the last of the curlers, threw the script down, and brushed out her hair.

"I can't believe you're auditioning for a soap opera," I said.

She sat down and sighed. "I know, I know. You don't have to remind me. No one has less respect for them than I do. But I have to be practical. Now that I've got a daughter to raise, I can't be so picky about my parts. If I get this job it'll mean lots of money. And from what I understand, this character will be a lead indefinitely. I've got to try for it."

She picked up the script and glanced at it. I walked over to the crib and looked down at Magda, a little over a year old. Jennifer picked up her purse, grabbed a sweater, and kissed my cheek. "You're a darling. I'll be back by five-thirty, six at the very latest. She'll probably just sleep, but if she wakes up just give her something to drink. I'll feed her when I get back."

She left and gently closed the door. I looked at Magda and watched her body move with her breathing. So peaceful and contented. Probably dreaming about ice cream, cup cakes, and the Three Bears.

Jennifer had decorated her apartment in a style I dubbed "late hippie." When she'd first moved in, that is. Mattress on the floor, pop star posters on the walls. A cable spool table with dripping candles. But since she'd given birth, everything had been replaced with inexpensive, but respectable mature people's furnishings. A sectional sofa, second-hand mahogany coffee table, a convertible bed, and reproductions of Degas, Cezanne, and Miro.

I sat down and opened the book I'd brought along. A sort of "experimental novel" published by a small press. It seemed to break every literary rule ever established. Parts were tedious, but others were funny in a macabre sort of way. I'm not sure how long I sat there reading when suddenly I heard a crash that sounded like a statuette shattering in the apartment next door. Jennifer had once told me that her neighbors fought all the time and threw things at each other. The noise was enough to awaken Magda, who was bawling and rubbing her eyes by the time I picked her up.

I brushed her little saffron ringlets off her forehead, kissed her cheek, and held her to my chest. She fastened her tiny arms around my neck and I patted her back saying, "There, there, everything's all right. Mommy will be home soon. She'll feed you and you can go back to your visions of sugar plums."

I think the sugar plums did it. She stopped crying and pulled back, scrutinizing my face. "It's me again," I said. "Remember me? I'm the one who always sings you to sleep, remember?"

She gurgled something that I was unable to decipher. I sat and held her on my knee, rocking her back and forth. She giggled. I tickled her chin and that made her laugh.

"Well, little Maggie, what shall we do 'til Mama comes home? We can go see a movie. There's a triple X-rated movie that just opened which I'm sure you'll just love." She burped.

I carried her to the sink and filled a glass with water, but she just pushed it away. We returned to the sofa. "How about some television? There's a rerun of *Gilligan's Island* starting in five minutes." She yawned and stretched. "No good, huh? I can read to you for a while." I scanned Jennifer's bookshelves. "What'll it be, Hemingway or Proust?" She started playing with my nose and hooked her finger inside my left nostril. "I know, you want to play." I placed her on the carpet and fetched some toys from her playpen. As I handed each one to her, she took it and flung it away. She laughed and clapped her hands together. I got down on my hands and knees and pretended I was a doggie. She seized my hair in her tiny hand and pulled as hard as she could. "Okay, you little monster," I chuckled, "you're going back to sleep." I gently placed her in the crib, pulled the coverlet up, and tucked it beneath her chin. Then I hummed an old Irish air until she fell asleep.

There is nothing as beautiful as a sleeping infant. The vulnerable serenity touches ones heart. A resting, living person that has not yet tasted the bitterness of life. Capable of growing up to be anything. Magda has more options than her mother or her godfather had. Jennifer and I will encourage her to explore them all.

I'd be willing to bet that the Aliens would adore Earth children. They may be repulsed or amused by adult humans, but kids would surely move them in the most positive of ways. Inspire goodwill. Make them see that perhaps Earthlings have some potential after all.

—— Chapter Six ——

During the four years I lived in Boston I fantasized about returning to New York, getting an apartment, and settling down to the serious business of becoming a professional musician. In the interim, my parents had fled the northern/urban life of complexity and severe seasonal changes, and planted roots in a small, comfortable town on the outskirts of Fort Lauderdale. The weather pleased them, the slower pace was simple to adjust to, and the golf course —just minutes from their front door—made their life irresistible.

Since I no longer had a home in New York to return to, I moved in—temporarily—with an aunt and uncle who lived in a huge apartment on the Upper West Side. I began to look for work. My chief priority was to generate an income that would cover the expense of a small apartment so I could establish some independence and keep the period of imposition on my relatives as brief as possible.

I found two part-time jobs rather quickly and saved enough money after three months to pay the first month's rent and security deposit on a tiny studio in the West Village.

I worked four days a week on the assembly line at an electronics factory which manufactured voltage converters.

For tourists traveling overseas who wanted to bring hair dryers, electric razors, and other appliances which were not compatible with European (and other foreign) wiring systems. I hated the work but it was fairly undemanding. I could let my mind wander and dream up ideas for new songs.

I also worked three nights a week at a record store. The amount of time spent trying to earn enough to pay the bills left little for writing, practicing, and auditioning. But I minimized all wastes of time and managed to perform at small clubs on the weekends, with just enough left for eating and sleeping. The dishes would frequently go unwashed for weeks and the dust began to accumulate in layers, but I considered that unimportant.

The record store job, however, turned out to be quite an education. Located on Eighth Street between Fifth and Sixth Avenues, it was a tri-level setup that stocked everything from bluegrass to opera. I was passing by one evening on my way to a folk club and noticed a sign that said "Wanted — Expert in Folk, Blues, and Country."

The manager, a beer-bellied pipe-smoker, leaned back behind his desk and asked if I'd answer several questions.

"What label does Joan Baez record for?"

"Used to be Vanguard, now it's A&M."

"Very good. Judy Collins?"

"Elektra. All of her records are on Elektra."

"I'm impressed. Is B. B. King a singer or guitarist?"

"Both. And a songwriter."

"What label has Muddy Waters recorded most of his classics for?"

"Chess."

"You're batting a thousand, kid. Who wrote " 'I'm So Lonesome I Could Cry'?"

"Hank Williams."

"Who's the hottest lady right now in country music?"

That was a toughie. I had no idea and decided to bluff. "Well, that's strictly a matter of opinion. Some say Dolly

63

Parton, some say Tammy Wynette, and some say Loretta Lynn. But as far as I'm concerned, none of 'em can touch Patsy Cline."

"Bullseye, kid. You got the job. You'll mainly be ordering new releases and working the floor, helping customers. When can you start?"

To me it was the continuation of my music education. I had never been exposed to any of the four female vocalists I'd mentioned, but had, of course, heard their names. So I immediately set out to listen to whatever country albums I could get my hands on and was able to tell one from another in no time at all. Eventually I became a fan and grew to love George Jones, Waylon Jennings, and Merle Haggard as well.

The other part of my education came from Deryck Washington, the classical expert at the store. My first night on the job, he walked over, shook my hand, and introduced himself. He had a closely-cropped Afro, mocha skin tone, and a firm physique.

"I take it you're the new folkie. I'm classical and opera."

"Pleased to meet you."

"A word of warning: Benny over there," he indicated a flabby guy in a flannel shirt with long, greasy hair, "hates anything that isn't jazz and he will give you a hard time. I, on the other hand, love folk music, so I welcome the opportunity to talk with you about it. The last guy didn't know anything. He was really a rocker and bluffed his way into the job. I hope you know your stuff."

Sometimes after work, Deryck and I would meet his wife, a striking Haitian woman named Lorna. The three of us would go to a bar and sip wine while talking about music. Lorna worked as a secretary, but was a singer too. Musical comedy was her primary interest.

Whenever I got duplicate promotional copies of folk albums I gave them to Deryck and when he got a recording that he didn't want to add to his collection, he'd give it to me. In this way I learned about Verdi, Stravinsky, Debussy, and Albeniz—familiar names but unfamiliar music. Deryck would commandeer the store's stereo system when we worked together and point out the differences in interpretation between versions of a piano sonata or a symphony. He'd compare one diva's high C to another, and hearing the different versions back to back was very illuminating.

In addition, I was able to keep abreast of all the latest rock and jazz recordings thanks to Benny, the jazzman, and Cathy, a heavyset girl with sea-green eyes, the rock expert. And Benny, once he realized I was receptive to Ellington and Coltrane, caged his hostility and treated me like an equal. But Deryck and Cathy, to whom jazz was mostly noise, often suffered the abuse of his acid tongue.

*

I had been seeing Mike about four nights a week for almost two months and decided it was time that he met Donald. He suggested that the three of us go to see *The Normal Heart*, a play about AIDS. Donald's lover had recently died of AIDS and I thought he would probably try to avoid such a painful confrontation, but he suggested it, so I got us tickets.

The structure of the evening worked in such a way that Mike and Donald established a rapport immediately. If we'd had dinner first and then seen the play, Mike would probably have been silent through the meal. But we attended the play first which provided us with a common topic for discussion. We ate at a place called Penelope's, a few blocks from the theater.

"What did you think?" I asked Donald after we'd ordered sandwiches and french fries.

"Powerful stuff. Everyone should see it."

"I'm still shaking," said Mike. "The production is spare enough so it doesn't direct attention away from the basic conflicts. And the playwright's way of looking at the larger issues, from the perspective of someone personally involved in the struggle, makes the message hit where it hurts."

"Can you believe it," I said, "all the nasty remarks about Mayor Koch?"

"He deserves it," said Donald. "He's so afraid of being labeled gay that he's really dragging his heels as far as financial allocations go."

"This is an important play," said Mike, "because it will probably enlighten a lot of people. Everyone perceives AIDS as a gay problem, but it won't be long before it starts turning up everywhere. The existence of bisexuals ensures it. As soon as straight people realize that they are in danger too, we'll see more action, more money, and I hope, more results."

"This play will definitely help spread the word," I said. "I'm going to tell everyone I know that it's a must see."

Mike and Donald agreed.

When the food arrived Mike filled Donald in about his set designing career and Donald informed Mike about his painting.

We went for a cocktail at the Corral after dinner. Two rounds later, Mike and I left. Donald said he wanted to cruise a bit before going home. We reminded him to be careful.

When Mike and I got into bed I was nervous about initiating sex. "I guess the play made me a bit skittish," I confessed.

"Me too. But we've already done everything we can do. At this stage, any possible damage has already been done."

"I don't want to die, but I don't want to become afraid of intimacy."

We tore into each other as though it might be our last time. Sweaty and spent, we fell asleep, his back curved into my chest, as close and tight as two teaspoons in a plush-lined silverware case.

*

If we get to the Alien's planet before they get here, it is entirely possible that this scenario may ensue.

A triumvirate of Earthlings—a Diplomat, an Industrialist, and a Militarist—will descend from a starship bearing,

66

as gifts, a black leather-bound Bible, and a roll of Kruger-rands. The startled Aliens will prepare their finest accommodations for the delegation from beyond the stars.

After a respectable amount of time, the Alien leader will greet his guests at a sumptuous reception. "Welcome, friends. We hope that you will find our atmosphere and nourishment to be compatible with your physiology." (A computer/translator will prevent any communications snafus.)

The Diplomat will steer the Alien leader into a corner and present a first edition of Proust, an ounce of cocaine, and a guidebook to the United Nations.

"What's a Proust?" The Alien will ask.

"I'll send you a copy of the Cliff Notes," says the Diplomat, reassuringly.

The Industrialist will intervene and ask the Alien to sign agreements allowing Toyota, McDonald's, and Sergio Valente first option for establishing spheres of influence on Alien soil. The Alien will look perplexed and the Industrialist — prepared for this eventuality — will offer a VCR and video cassette which explains the importance of ground transportation, fast food, and designer clothing.

"What is a designer jean?" the Alien will implore.

The Industrialist slaps his fat, blue-jeaned ass and says, "Sex appeal," with a leering wink.

The Alien will blush and say, "I see."

Next the Militarist will command the Alien's attention and offer to give a lecture tour to instruct the Alien inhabitants in crowd control, bureaucracy, bribery, and torture as a means of communication.

"What is torture?" the Alien will ask.

"Friendly persuasion," will be the Militarist's answer.

Two years later, the Aliens are at war with their nearest neighboring planet, their world is crisscrossed with littered, pockmarked highways dotted with billboards and sex motels, the suicide rate has tripled, and all the preschoolers are named Alexis or Rocky.

*

I was watching the news on television last night and some rabbi was being interviewed. He said that homosexuality was an affront to God, that AIDS patients and all known homosexuals should be quarantined, and that the gay high school in New York should be closed down.

I turned off the tube, smoked a joint, and thought about this. And the more I thought, the angrier I got.

I resent anyone espousing a personal opinion as though they were speaking for anyone else. Especially if the anyone else is me. The President, for example, commits countless atrocities every day as a representative of the American people. I'm an American and he doesn't represent my point of view. Not ever. Must I renounce my citizenship to free myself of the blame? What can I say to a Central American refugee whose family and property have been destroyed? "I didn't vote for him so even though I'm an American I'm not responsible for your problems." I pity the refugee and curse the President for perpetrating criminal acts in my name.

But the rabbi really gets to me because there is no logic in his proposal. Let's say, for the sake of argument, that God exists. I don't believe it, but let's pretend for a moment. The rabbi claims that, according to God, homosexuality should not exist. This makes no sense. If God — who supposedly created earth and everything in it — doesn't want there to be gay people, why are we everywhere and why have we always been so? These are questions, however, that the rabbi is never asked. Nor does he chance any speculation.

But what really gets to me is how can a man who supposedly represents a group of people who were persecuted by the millions less than fifty years ago, take it upon himself to persecute anyone else? Are holocausts self-perpetuating?

If presidents and rabbis can commit criminal acts in my name, then I must disassociate myself from them. I can no longer be an American Jew. I must be a nameless glob of protoplasm crawling around the planet, trying to survive and not get in the way of the other globs of protoplasm trying to survive, crawling around the planet. But I think it would be a lot better and easier if we were all just Earthlings and could learn to leave each other alone. Unless an opinion is solicited. Or assistance requested. Otherwise keep your hands off and your mouth shut.

*

I met Amos at the airport and carried two of his four suitcases out to the taxi. Flushed and excited, I was giddy because it had taken twenty-seven years for me to find what I believed was true love. Amos was as sweet as could be. He gave me several orchids, hydroponically grown. We hugged and kissed in the taxi all the way into Manhattan and I told him all of the plans I'd made. Dinner reservations for that evening, theater tickets for the following week, and a party at Donald's so Amos could meet our friends.

We lugged his baggage up the four flights of stairs to our new apartment overlooking Sheridan Square. Before he unpacked, we stripped and made love.

The next day he announced that he was going job hunting and would follow up the leads he'd collected from New Orleans restaurant folk. He arrived home that evening in jubilant spirits. "I have an interview tomorrow with the manager of Cafe In The Park and I get the impression they need waiters desperately. And I'm sure they'll find my resume impressive."

"A job on your first day. This calls for a celebration." I broke out the coke I'd bought from Max for just this occasion and we each snorted two lines.

"I didn't get the job yet," he said and eagerly vacuumed two more lines.

The first week went better than I expected. He got the job, with a good balance of lunch and dinner shifts. We went to Donald's party and Amos met Ed, Frannie, and her circle of pretty boys. The party was a grand success and I was deliriously happy.

I expected that Amos might be a bit homesick for New Orleans and watched for any overt signs (covert ones too), but he seemed to be content with New York and me. There was no indication that I should think otherwise.

*

Donald and I had talked about pooling our interests, trying to see if we could collaborate on some artistic project. He would attempt to illustrate some of my stories and I would try to create stories from his sketches and paintings. It was an idea that we had discussed many times. But we'd never actually done anything about it. He phoned me one night and made arrangements to come by so we could transform the conjecture into something concrete.

It was early evening when he arrived. I buzzed him in and we kissed at the door. He looked tired and thin. Removing his jacket, he sighed and plopped down on the couch. I fixed two mugs of coffee and amaretto.

"You look awful," I said, "have you been eating and sleeping like a normal person should?"

"Not really. I think I have AIDS."

He waited for my sympathy but I was in short supply. "Have you been to your doctor?"

"Not yet. I probably got it from Lorenzo."

"There are plenty of people who've been in contact with the virus who haven't gotten it themselves."

"It's hopeless."

"Only if you refuse to take care of yourself."

"I'm gonna die anyway."

"We're all gonna die anyway. Not eating or sleeping will only make it happen sooner."

He looked away and shook his head. Then sipped from his mug. "How are you?"

"I was fine until you arrived. If you came over just to make me worry about you, you've succeeded. I thought we were going to start putting a book together."

"I don't want to die."

"Good. Neither do I. Let's forget about death and talk about words and images."

He handed me a folder of sketches. I gave him a sheaf of stories. He began reading and I scanned a few drawings.

"Do you think we should go over this now," I asked, "or work on it when we're alone?"

"I can't concentrate with someone else around. Why don't we give ourselves a couple of weeks to see what we can get from each other's stuff, then get together and look at the results?"

"Sounds good to me," I said, placing his portfolio next to the typewriter.

"Let's get stoned," he said, wielding a long, thick joint.

"Twist my arm."

He walked to the record shelf and pulled out *The Lester Young Story*. "Can we listen to this?"

"Of course." I cued the record and he lit the joint. We spent several hours listening to Young's silky/smokey sax lines. Then gorged ourselves on pasta at the Trattoria a few blocks away.

*

I've seen the movie of *Gypsy* and I've heard all of the horror stories about stage parents and the sad plight of Jackie Coogan, but I never thought a great deal about child actors until I started working at the box office. Then the subject became inescapable.

Approximately one out of every ten shows that we handle has a kid or several in the cast. It didn't take long to realize that although some kids are ambitious all by themselves, most are driven by a parent or parents who either have dreams of glory and riches, or are themselves failed thespians who expect their offspring to accomplish what they could not.

I remember in particular one case that I found horribly distressing. The child was a boy of about eight. I'll call him Tommy. He was bright and adorable, a perfect example of what a child actor is expected to be. The kind of whom aunts say, "He's gonna break a lot of hearts."

"He can be anything he wants to be," say the uncles.

Tommy had a small role in a wacky comedy in which he was supposed to play a spoiled brat. This he did, marvelously. And it was pure acting as far as I could tell, because offstage he was as well mannered and nice as any kid I've ever known.

His mother, however, was an alcoholic. We never found out if Tommy's father abandoned them, was driven away, or had died. But we felt sorry for Tommy and his mother, living without benefit of a mature male.

Mrs. Jones would drop Tommy off a half hour before curtain and would sometimes return at the end of the last act, sometimes not. But she always arrived in a drunken stupor. If she had not yet returned by the time he'd changed, he'd sit patiently in the lobby and talk to us, never once complaining about his mother's condition. She would stagger in eventually, hurling verbal abuse at anyone she encountered. Tommy would look away and pretend not to notice, then dutifully follow her home.

On the occasions when she arrived before the final curtain, the house manager would invariably have to ask her to keep quiet, as she sat — drinking from a bottle in a bag — creating as much noise as possible.

When the show closed we learned that Tommy's income was their sole support. And though he never expressed any displeasure with his work, neither was he the gung ho type who seems to thrive on it. Just a quiet, polite boy who did what he was told.

We are currently handling a show that has several youngsters in the cast, and I've been dealing with their mothers on a daily basis. One, in particular whom I'll call Mrs. Smith. I've not yet seen Mrs. Smith interacting with her daughter, nor have I observed her to be anything other than sober, but I have been witness to her manipulative manner.

She came to the box office with eyes so wide and a smile so phony it was difficult to take her seriously.

"How do you do today?" she trilled.

"Just fine, Ma'am, and yourself?"

"Oh, my life is glorious."

"Glad to hear it."

"I want seventeen tickets for opening night, ten as close up as you can get them, four comps, eight at staff rate, and I'll pay full price for the rest."

"I'm sorry, Mrs. Smith, but opening night tickets are reserved for critics, producers, and agents."

"But my daughter is in the cast."

"Yes, I know."

"She's got the leading role!"

"That doesn't alter the ticket availability."

"I have twelve members of my family, five on my side and seven on my husband's, who are coming all the way from Montreal just for this occasion."

"There's nothing I can do."

"But I already told them I'd get tickets!"

"What can I say? There aren't any to be had."

"I'm the mother of the star."

"I know that."

"And all my relatives are coming. I'll be so embarrassed." The tears began to trickle from the corners of her eyes.

"I'm terribly sorry."

"Well," she said with stoic reserve, "I guess I have a problem."

She walked away looking as though I'd struck her with a sledgehammer. Of course I feel guilty at not being able to fulfill her request. I hate seeing anyone cry. I wonder if she turns on the tears to get her daughter to do things she doesn't want to do. A child need not be battered to be abused.

I've not yet encountered a stage father. That they are probably just as bad, I willingly concede.

——— Chapter Seven ———

Prior to the time I applied for a job at the box office, in addition to working at the record store, I was employed by an electronics firm. Located in a large industrial building on Park Avenue South, the company occupied an entire floor that was divided into three areas: office space, assembly, and shipping. The office contained a private room for the boss — to which I never gained entry — and a more accessible space with three desks. Behind these sat a bookkeeper, secretary, and receptionist. Beyond the office was an enormous area with stock piled in the center and assembly tables running around the perimeter. At the far end was the shipping table — laden with empty cartons, postage scales, and stamp machines — adjacent to the entrance to the service elevators.

Sitting or standing at the tables were people of all ages, sizes, and colors. The people at the left wall assembled the voltage converters, the people at the right wall tested them, sorting out the acceptable units from the duds. I was at the tables in the rear, stuffing the converters and instruction pamphlets into brightly-colored display boxes.

A large radio broadcasted music to all the workers from its position on top of a stack of shipping cartons. Every morning people would argue over which station would be listened to that day. Some only wanted to hear rock, others soul, still others classical. I didn't much care because I hardly paid attention. I kept a pad and pen in my shirt pocket and would daydream until I'd come up with an idea for a song lyric or a short story. I'd dash to the water fountain in the reception area, or to the men's room and jot down my idea.

One day the foreman came over to me. A squat, flabby man with bushy eyebrows.

"You know," he said, "if you didn't drink so much water, you wouldn't have to go to the bathroom so often."

"Gee," I said, feigning ignorance, "I never thought of that."

"We've got to keep our production levels up and you leave the line more than anyone."

"That's true," I admitted, "but I also work faster than any of the other boxers."

He glanced at the guy sitting next to me who moved through life like a film in slow motion.

"You're right," he finally admitted and never again mentioned my drinking or bathroom habits.

*

Donald called last night and asked if I'd seen the season premiere of *Dynasty*.

"Well, yes," I admitted.

"Did you like it?"

"Well, no. I used to enjoy it because it was so trashy, but now I can't get past the bad writing and horrible acting. Either I'm getting more sophisticated or the show is getting worse. I don't think I'll watch it again."

"Most people think that if they like something it must be good, if they don't it's bad. But you and I know it's not that simple," he said. "I don't like Rembrandt, but I acknowledge his talent. And I adore Marvel comics, though I know they have as much value as a Twinkie has vitamins."

"What gets me," I said, "is the numbers. I'd estimate that about seventy-five percent of America saw *Dynasty* last night, and of that group, probably about ninety-five percent thought they were watching quality work because they responded to it in a positive way. But most of those people have not been in a bookstore or a library since high school, so they have no way of separating good writing from bad."

"Or galleries or museums," said Donald. "Why do we knock ourselves out being creative, trying to do something exceptional when most people won't even bother to look at it or read it and of those that do, few will have any real appreciation."

I said, "I don't know. Why do we persist?"

"Vanity, narcissism."

"Glory," I added, "prestige."

"Certainly not for the *money*," he chortled.

And the next thing I knew we were talking about gay writers. We'd both just read *Moby Dick* and were convinced that Herman Melville was gay.

"He had to be to write a book like that," I said.

Donald agreed. "There's enough gay sensibility to make Quentin Crisp blush. Like the scene where the guys are in bed together."

"What about the sperm scene," I interjected.

This went on for a while. And then somehow the focus switched from Melville to Henry James.

"A closet case for sure," said Donald.

I agreed. "If he were alive today . . ."

"If he were alive today," said Donald, "he'd be a *very* old queen."

*

We said goodbye to September yesterday. It's cooler now. The few days of autumn sandwiched between the slow, humid summer and the endless freezing winter are like furloughs between death-defying battles. Just enough of a reward, a taste of hope, to lure you back to the trenches and bolster your sense of duty. A brief respite from the front allows you to imagine that winning the war is not only possible but worth the effort.

So I seize the days of autumn with pleasure, ignoring all of the beckoning demands. I notice the sun on the leaves of the trees, creating jewels and shadows among the up-stretched branches that flaunt shimmering greenery like bracelets. The passersby — their running shorts and tanktops packed away now — are all in jerseys and sweaters that reflect the efforts of fashion designers. If summer and winter wear is all too prosaic, bowing to the dictates of comfort and protection, then the brief periods of autumn and spring provide the only opportunity for clothing that is wholly aesthetic and not at the mercy of necessity.

"Autumn and spring are the only times that New Yorkers can be truly fashionable," Mike remarked the other day. And the congested sidewalks below cheerfully support his claim.

*

On the night we'd met, Amos had referred to a brother that lived in New York, but he'd never mentioned him again. That is, until we'd been living together for about a week. One evening after I'd returned from the factory, he announced that we were invited to dinner the following Friday at his brother and sister-in-law's Upper East Side apartment.

We stepped out of the elevator onto the sixth floor and Amos led me to #6F. He pressed the buzzer and the door opened a few moments later.

"It's Amos and his lover," the diminutive, redheaded woman shouted over her shoulder. She kissed Amos and shook my hand. "We've heard so much about you. I'm Gloria. Let me take your jackets."

I smiled, removed my jacket, and handed it to her as she ushered us out of the hall and into the living room. Whatever wall space was not occupied by large oil paintings was dotted with South Sea Island masks (whether originals or replicas, I had no idea). The high-tech furniture sat on a white pile carpet. Track lights illuminated the large room with diagonal shafts of brightness.

"Matthew is making a salad in the kitchen and Christopher has just gone to bed. Let me see if he's asleep yet."

She turned and left the room as Amos and I seated ourselves before a plexiglass and chrome coffee table with two enormous ceramic ashtrays. A moment later Gloria returned, leading a beautiful blond boy who stared at the floor. He glanced at Amos and I, then started bawling.

"Hush now, Christopher. These are your two uncles who live downtown and they came all the way up in the subway to see you."

Unimpressed, the child cried on. I smiled at Gloria and she smiled back, just as Amos' brother entered the room. A tall, burly man with dark hair and a mustache, he shook Amos' hand, then mine. "I'm Matthew and I've heard so much about you."

He released my hand, picked up the wailing tot. "C'mon, Li'l Nipper," he said, and carried the boy back to his bedroom.

"Would you like a drink?" Gloria inquired.

"I'd *love* one," drawled Amos.

"Me too."

"We've got scotch, vodka, gin—"

"Scotch on the rocks," said Amos.

"I'll have the same."

She fixed the drinks, placed them on coasters before us, and fetched a platter with paté, cheese, crackers, and a small dish of mustard. Dijon. Amos made a paté, cheese, and mustard sandwich, handed it to me, then made one for himself. Gloria sat down next to Amos, brushed the hair off his forehead and said, "You've lost weight. We'll fix that." She glanced at her wristwatch. "Dinner will be ready in about a half hour." She patted my arm. "Amos tells us you're a musician."

"That's right."

"How's it going?" Although Matthew's accent was deep south, just like Amos', Gloria's speech betrayed her midwestern upbringing.

"Well, it's never easy," I laughed. "Basically, I'm performing my own songs, accompanying myself on guitar and piano, at a couple of clubs in the village. But I'm trying to get a band together, so we can record some demo tapes."

"That sounds wonderful!" she said with far more enthusiasm than I thought the reply merited.

She turned to Amos. "And how are things at Cafe In The Park?"

"Not bad. But I have to wait 'til I've been there longer so I can get more dinner shifts. The lunch crowd doesn't tip enough."

Matthew reappeared. "How about some music?" Without waiting for a reply, he slapped a Stanley Turrentine album on the turntable, fixed drinks for Gloria and himself, and sat.

"Amos tells us you're a musician."

I grinned at Gloria and repeated the same speech I'd just delivered.

"What do you think of Stanley Turrentine?"

"He's great," I said, "but this record is too overarranged for my taste. His earlier stuff was funkier—he doesn't need all those violins and synthesizers."

Matthew looked stung and I hated myself for being honest about music with a nonmusician. I filed the incident in my brain under Being More Tactful In The Future.

And so the evening progressed. Amos was unusually quiet. I guess he was as nervous as I was. The food—shrimp cocktails, green salad, roast beef with new potatoes and asparagus, peach melba—was superb. And Gloria and Matthew did everything they could to communicate to me that they accepted me as Amos' lover and wanted to see us often.

When we left I was overjoyed. I liked Matthew and Gloria, looked forward to watching Christopher grow up, and was thrilled that our union had been blessed by Amos' relatives.

*

While performing one night at a small folk-rock club on Bleecker Street I met a girl who sang like a siren and played fiddle like the devil. She was born and raised in North Carolina and had come to New York to become a rock star.

It was a Friday night—I didn't have to work at the factory the next day—so I was in a fairly good mood when the time came for my last set. Laura came over to me right before I went on.

"I caught your last set," she said, clutching her violin case to her breast, "and wondered if you wanted to jam a little on the next one."

Her honey blonde hair haloed a starchy complexion and flashing green eyes, her bosom threatened to sever her black halter top. The faded jeans were embroidered with an assortment of birds and flowers.

"I'm doing my own stuff," I said, "but maybe there are a couple of pop tunes we both know."

"You know 'Honky Tonk Women' by the Stones?" she asked.

"Yup, do you know 'Peaceful Easy Feeling' by the Eagles?"

"Yes," she drawled, as though the word had two syllables.

About halfway through my set, I brought her onstage and introduced her. We played the two agreed upon songs. Her fiddle breaks and pretty harmony blended perfectly with my style.

That night before falling asleep, I pictured us together as a regular performing duet and realized that if I could bring out her natural country roots, we could have a viable act. I phoned her the next day and asked if she'd like to get together to jam and talk over some possibilities.

Her primary musical interests were Fleetwood Mac and Steely Dan.

"Have you ever sung any Dolly Parton songs?"

"Sheeit, no. That's what my parents listen to."

"You want to make some money playing music?"

"Yes, I do."

I loaned her some albums by various female country artists, suggested some songs that she might learn, and made a date to get together in a week.

At first she was hesitant to express her affinity for country, but I kept telling her that she should develop her skills in country — if only to earn some money — and she could rock out whenever she wanted until she could afford to leave the country behind. She reluctantly acquiesced.

I learned a few songs by George Jones, Waylon Jennings, and Merle Haggard and, before long, we had a repertoire of over twenty-five songs consisting mainly of country hits and a few quasi-country numbers that I'd written.

We began to attract some attention and word got around that we wanted to form a band. A drummer, bassist, and pedal-steel guitarist started rehearsing with us and we got some gigs at classier clubs for more money. This was just after the success of *Urban Cowboy* and New Yorkers were suddenly discovering cowboy boots, Texas two-steps, and mechanical bulls.

We called ourselves High In The Saddle and we were the most unlikely country combo ever formed: an Italian pedal-steel player from Brooklyn; a Hispanic drummer, Chico Valentin, from the Bronx; a jazz bassist from Montreal; and a Jewish, not to mention gay, singer/guitarist from Long Island. Laura was the only member with real country roots, and she was the one who always needed coaxing. The rest of us loved playing country because it was so exotic to us. To her it was the same old thing that she'd come to

New York to escape. But she persevered. And eventually became quite an accomplished bluegrass fiddler. Her "Orange Blossom Special" would, in fact, steal the show every night. But her heart was never in it. She eventually left us to join a rock group and High In The Saddle was no longer in demand without the sexy female fiddler. We disbanded and went our separate musical ways.

I don't know what Laura's doing now. But so far, she has not attained the kind of success that she dreamed about. I'm convinced, though, that had she pursued a career in country, she'd be the toast of Nashville.

*

Another friend just died of AIDS. His name was Arthur and he was a journalist who specialized in political analyses and literary reviews. He was a real fighter. While some guys diagnosed with AIDS just give up and wait for death, Arthur saw every doctor in town. He tried all the possible treatments from macrobiotics to chemotherapy. Rather than cut himself off from people, he stayed in touch until the end.

When we'd met, he was a strapping bodybuilder — the best pecs and lats I'd ever seen. When he died, he was a mere remnant. I watched his body wither and fade, but his mind remained sharp, his spirit more determined than ever before.

When I die — whether from AIDS or whatever — that is how I want to go. I will not give up.

*

After running into Jennifer at Max's, we fell into a regular routine of dinner, conversation, and attending each other's performances. She'd get me comps to her shows and I'd put her on the guest list at the clubs where I worked. And when we broke up with boyfriends, we'd introduce each other to prospective new beaux.

I once set her up with a keyboard player I was working with. His name was Allan and he seemed to be less concerned with macho posturing than many of the musicians I knew. He liked theater, so I got tickets for them and arranged a blind date. They saw each other a few times and had great sex, Jennifer told me. And then it fizzled. I asked her what went wrong and she dropped by one afternoon to talk about it. We sat by the window overlooking the park and passed a joint back and forth. The sun picked up the highlights in her hair — long and straight, at the time — and she looked relaxed and comfortable in a baggy sweater and khaki trousers.

"The problem," she said, "is not so much that Allan regards women as sex objects, just that his only interest is physical beauty. It's not that he's threatened by women who are intelligent or ambitious, it's just that he thinks if a woman is less than a knockout, she's somehow second rate."

"Why should that bother you? You're a knockout."

"So he told me," she said drily. "It's the remarks he makes about other women that bother me. We were out at a restaurant last week and at the next table were two average-looking women. I could tell by the bits of conversation I overheard that they were intelligent, interesting people. And you know what he said to me?" She didn't wait for me to respond. " 'Can you imagine going to bed with a woofer like that? I'd have to put a bag over her head, or I'd throw up.' "

"Maybe that's his silly way of paying you a compliment."

"How can I accept a compliment from someone who thinks that the sum total of a human being is in their bone structure and complexion? It frightens me. Suppose I were to get serious about this guy. At the first crowsfoot, blemish, or extra pound, he'd drop me like a hot potato."

"Well, you know," I said, "it's typical of all males. Most of the gay guys I know are obsessed with looks. They develop their bodies while their brains go unattended and are always on the lookout for Mr. Hot Stuff. They don't care about personality or intelligence. Just pretty faces, perfect bodies, and fashionable clothing."

"You know, you're right," she said. "Now that I think about it. I always thought that gay and straight people were so different. But I guess gay men and straight men have more in common with each other, and straight women and lesbians too. Men are attracted by good looks. Women tend to look deeper. I've known women who have lovers, male or female, who are not that attractive physically, but whose hearts and personalities made them what we call a good catch. And not in the financial sense."

"You're right," I agreed. "Remember that guy you dated for a while, Walter? He was not a beauty, but he was a wonderful person. The two of you got along like a dream team."

"Too bad he wanted to get married and have children right away."

"And stupid me, pining away for Harry the Hunk who never treated me like I deserved, but I was always ready for his abuse, just so I could have sex with a bona fide stud."

"You'll learn," she said. "You'll meet a guy who'll sweep you off your feet on the strength of his personality. Not like Amos," she laughed.

"Not to change the subject or anything, but I was wondering, do you want to have a kid or kids someday?"

"Yes," she said slowly. "But only when I'm ready. And you'll be the kid's fairy godfather."

"Watch it."

"I'm serious. I want my children to be free from prejudice. I want them to grow up knowing all kinds of people so when they're finally out on their own, the range of humanity won't be such a shock. You know what I mean. Our parent's generation raised us in little ghettos. When I met my first black person I was terrified. And I thought all lesbians were going to try to seduce me. It took me a while to feel comfortable around different kinds of people. Will you be my kid's pseudo-uncle?"

"Of course."

"Besides," she grinned, "what if my kid turns out to be gay?"

"There's always that possibility."

"Well, I want you around. You'd be the perfect role model."

"Gosh, I don't know what to say. Flatterer."

*

I am completely lacking in patience. I want everything to happen now. Every time I'm expecting something — a letter, a check, a magazine that's accepted one of my stories — I drive myself crazy until it arrives. I leap out of bed and run to the mailbox. There's nothing but junk; sales circulars, offers to purchase magazine subscriptions, press releases for performance artists.

I'd rather receive a letter stating that my article, story, or manuscript has been rejected, than wait another day to find out that it's been accepted. (I know that sounds dumb, but once something is rejected at least I can send it elsewhere. Sitting around waiting makes me feel powerless.)

A letter written personally to me is like proof that I exist. On the days when I receive only junk mail or nothing at all, a maddening silence descends that evokes the loneliness and isolation of a sensory deprivation tank.

When I receive a letter from a friend, a check for an article, a note from a publisher, it's like a Klaxon blaring. A cannon roaring. Yes, I'm alive and there are others out there who are aware of it. It smashes the solitude. I feel better.

I'm about to go down to my mailbox. Will this turn out to be a boring or exciting day?

Only my mailman knows for sure.

—— Chapter Eight ——

I had been witness to many marriages prior to my receiving the invitation to Chico Valentin's wedding and bachelor party. But they were usually large family affairs, most often cousins of mine. The ceremonies were always strictly religious rituals with rabbis playing their parts as though coached by Stanislavsky. And the receptions were grand and ostentatious with over two hundred guests, twelve-piece bands, photographers, and several acres worth of floral arrangements. But I'd never been invited to a bachelor party, so when Chico's invitation arrived I responded affirmatively that Mike and I would gladly attend.

The bachelor party was held at Chico's loft on West Fourteenth Street. A huge, formerly industrial site that had been converted into a rehearsal space and living area. Upon entering, one passed a drum booth and huge sound baffles. Then passed through a thick wooden door to a studio apartment with stove, refrigerator, and cabinets occupying one wall, a waterbed with multicolored afghan in one corner and four long sofas surrounding a coffee table that stood in the center of the room. The air was thick with marijuana smoke. An enormous video screen had been suspended from the ceiling and a horde of men — mostly musicians whom I'd either met or played with at one time or another — were hanging around talking excitedly about who'd been signed to which label, who'd been dropped by which label, and who had gotten the position of Joe Rockstar's lead guitarist.

On the coffee table, surrounded by a motley collection of ashtrays, was a large, circular mirror with thick lines of cocaine that spelled out CON RATU ATIONS CHICO. The G and L were already gone when we arrived.

I introduced Mike to everyone I knew. I looked for Russell, or any of the other Revulsionz, but they were not in attendance. I subsequently found out that Chico had left the band, and not on the best of terms.

We fetched cocktails from the self-service bar set up in the kitchen area and sat down to watch the video screen. A skinny, blonde girl was attempting to swallow the biggest penis I've ever seen. Mike looked away in embarrassment. I was afraid to look away, lest I be labeled a wimp. A fear I'd developed while still a believer in the music business.

Chico came over and shook our hands. His black hair — all ringlets and curls — looked wet and shiny. His road map eyes betrayed his highness. He was dressed like a pimp, in a lime shirt, orange trousers, and patent leather shoes. "Hey, guys, really glad you could come," he smiled effusively.

"What's Linda doing while you're kissing your freedom goodbye?"

"The girls are having their own party tonight over at Judy's — she's Lionel's girlfriend."

"I don't suppose they rented a screen and porn videos," said Mike.

"Dunno," said Chico. "Their party is as much of a secret to us as ours is to them."

He excused himself and Mike and I sampled the coke as various former bandmates came over to chat.

"I hear you're writing music reviews," said Brooks, a bass player I used to hang out with after rehearsals.

"That's right."

"Even though it's a gay paper and my band's straight, would you check us out sometime and write it up?"

"Sure."

"We need all the exposure we can get."

"Just send me a press release."

"Great."

Irwin, a trumpet player — obviously drunk — tottled over and placed a hand on Mike's shoulder. "I just heard a good one, wanna hear it?"

"Okay," Mike said.

"What's the difference between a girl and a toilet?"

A look of disgust crept over Mike's face.

"I don't think we want to know," I said.

"But it's really good," Irwin insisted.

"Okay," I said, uneasily, "what's the difference between a girl and a toilet?"

"A toilet doesn't follow you around saying 'I love you' after you've used it."

"That's gross," said Mike.

"The worst," I agreed.

We left a few minutes later.

The wedding took place the next day at Chico's mother and father-in-law's on the Upper West Side. It was much nicer than the bachelor party. Nothing elaborate, just a simple buffet. Nothing religious, just a civil service.

Mike and I had a very pleasant time at the wedding. However, I don't think we'll be attending any more bachelor parties.

*

I felt so good after meeting Amos' brother, sister-in-law, and nephew that I was willing to let a lot of things go by. Amos was a study in bad habits and it was not unusual for him to leave the apartment and forget to turn off the faucet or the bathroom light. Once he forgot to lock the door. Any one of these transgressions would ordinarily have made me lose my temper, but I attributed all of his behavior to his getting used to living in New York.

Time went by but things did not get any better. After his fourth week here, he began to recoil from my sexual advances. I thought it was a phase we had to go through. Like a rite of passage. After two weeks of no sexual contact, I waited up for him one night. I intended to talk with him and ask if anything was wrong.

But he never came home that night. Or the next.

At first I was frantic. My initial thought was that something terrible had happened to him. After the first night, I called every hospital in Manhattan to see if Amos was an accident victim. The response was negative.

In a panic, I called Donald and asked him what I should do.

"Call the restaurant and see if he showed up at work last night and leave a message for him to call you when he gets there tonight."

This I did. Yes, he'd worked last night. Yes, he'd get my message.

But by ten o'clock that evening I still hadn't heard anything.

I called Jennifer.

"Whatever you do, don't call him at work," she said. "He'll think you're checking up on him. He's probably just feeling his oats. He'll come back. You'll see."

The next morning, Gloria called. After telling me how much she enjoyed meeting me, she suggested that Amos and I come over some afternoon so we could see Christopher when he wasn't sleepy.

"That would be very nice," I said nervously, hoping she wouldn't ask to speak to Amos.

"Is Amos there?"

"He's, uh, out. Shopping," I lied.

"Would you please have him call us as soon as he gets back?"

"Of course."

Amos slithered in at eight o'clock the next morning and stretched out on the couch. His clothes were all rumpled, his hair greasy, and his eyes looked watery. I was getting ready to leave for the factory.

"Where have you been?" I asked, trying to conceal my anger.

"Around."

"I thought you were lying dead somewhere."

"I'm fine," he sneered.

"The next time you could at least call. I had to lie to Gloria to cover for you. Don't put me in that position ever again."

He sighed. As though he'd heard it before. If he had, it wasn't from me.

"Oh, by the way," I said, "I have to send in the rent next week. Just thought I'd give you fair warning."

"I've been meaning to tell you about that," he grinned.

"I'm listening."

"Things have been very slow at the restaurant. Tips are next to nothing. I don't think I'll have it all."

"I think I can cover it this time," I said, feeling protective and loving again. "Call Gloria."

I leaned over to kiss him goodbye but he turned his head away.

I was already late for work and nearly killed myself to get there on time.

I forgot about his cool attitude by the time I arrived to stuff converters into display boxes.

*

It had never occurred to me that I might someday quit the music business, but one day I evaluated my progress. I'd finally gotten four songs published and I was performing fairly regularly. But I could never make enough money to live on and was still relying on the factory and record store to pay my bills.

I had picked up a copy of a new, gay newspaper that was starting to appear at the newsstands. In it there was a message printed on the last page in which the editor explained the need for gay arts critics. I can become a music critic, I thought to myself, while sorting out my prospects. So I called the editor, told him I was a musician, and asked if I could write a sample record review.

"Are you gay?" he asked.

"Only in bed."

He chuckled and said I should write something and call him to arrange an interview.

I showed up a week later with a handful of record reviews. He read them while I sat there and thumbed through a copy of the newspaper. He finished, looked up, and smiled. "Would you be interested in covering a performance by Meg Christian next week?"

"Who's Meg Christian?"

"A lesbian folksinger."

"Sure," I said, and left the office with two tickets to the concert.

I called Jennifer that evening. "Guess what?"

"You're pregnant."

"Nope, I'm going to be a music critic."

"No shit?"

I told her about the interview and she seemed pleased. "You must show me a copy of the review as soon as it's published," she said. "Now you guess what."

"You're starring in a Broadway show?"

"Nope."

"You're starring in a Hollywood movie?"

"Nope."

"You're starring in a network TV series?"

"Three strikes and you're out. I just met this wonderful guy."

"Do tell."

"Well, I was having dinner with Sarah Longworth. She and I are appearing in a new comedy called *Hell's Belles* — it's the worst but it pays. Anyway, we were eating at Sushi's and this gorgeous guy comes over to say hello to Sarah and we're introduced. As soon as he leaves she says, 'He likes you, want a date?' So I said, 'Why not?' So she called him and he called me and I've seen him twice now and it's been wonderful."

"Tell me more."

"His name is Larry, he's a computer programmer, and he's handsome and sweet."

"Sounds great."

"And he's so romantic! On our first date he brought me one white rose. Could you die? And on the second he brought me a teddy bear with a note that said, 'I hope Teddy will remind you of me when I'm not around.' "

"Sweet dreams are made of this," I said. "Just don't rush into anything and make a fool of yourself like I did with Amos."

"No one could ever be as evil as that asshole," she said.

"You're probably right."

We said goodbye and I put down the receiver. About ten seconds later the phone rang. I was certain that it was Jennifer calling because she'd forgotten to tell me something.

"Jen?"

"No, sugar. It's darkmeat."

"Max, is that you?"

"Who else? Butterfly McQueen?"

"How are you?"

"Just fine. Listen, I was wondering if you could come over tomorrow night and check out my new act. I respect your opinion in these matters."

"Of course. What time?"

"Etiquette class gets out at 9:30. Can you be here at ten?"

"No problem."

Anyone who tries to be creative in this prosaic world has a tough task. Aside from the personal satisfaction that is attained, there are three possible rewards: money, fame, prestige. Somehow, even if your goal is only one of these, the other two always seem to follow. Still, a mere fraction of those who attempt to succeed artistically ever make it. And the wear and tear on one's soul sometimes makes the effort futile.

The thing is, you never know what you're getting until you get it. And arriving at the halfway point places you in the position of being neither here nor there. You're not yet an item, you're not yet a has-been, you're sort of like a never-was, even though you've been killing yourself to get some recognition.

Like a mountain climber, you look down and can only see part of the way from which you came. The view is blocked by rocks and ledges that obscure parts of the path you've already conquered. When you look up, most of the time you can barely see where you're going. Total darkness, blinding sunlight, or confusing shadows meet your gaze and fail to tell you anything you do not already know. You are aware that there is a pinnacle, but you have no idea what it looks like.

What will you do when you get there? Take a look around. Carve your name and the date into something solid. Try to make your way back down. And tell everyone it was worth it. The pain, despair, pleasure, and triumph. Yes, you'd do it again. And that's when you realize what your next project must be: find another mountain to climb. Anything else would be too dull.

*

Customers and stage mothers are only a part of the problem at Ticket Pandemonium. The clients—most of them, anyway—whose shows we handle are an entirely different sort of pain.

Broadway productions are too costly and risky for producers to get very far unless they know exactly what they are doing. Inept producers don't fool anyone for very long. But in the realm of off-Broadway, clowns and fools can masquerade as producers for quite some time until they are found out. These are the kinds of clients who make up a large percentage of our business.

And they come in droves. Would-be actors and directors who do not have the luck or talent to work on Broadway, write themselves pathetic scripts and set themselves up as producers. Then they arrive at the box office without a clue as to what they are getting into. And we innocent treasurers would be fired if we ever tried to talk any of them out of it. So we take them on as clients—knowing that their production will run less than two weeks and play to mostly empty houses. And lots of money will be lost. Off-Broadway is the arena for avant garde creative types to experiment. But boring vanity productions dominate the scene.

A smiling actor-type arrives at the door and holds out his hand.

"Hi, my name is Ned Bly and I'm producing a play at the Eighth Avenue Playhouse. I'd like to use your box office service."

"Please come in. Won't you sit down. What's the name of the play?"

"*Adam & Eve.*"

"Great title," I practically choke on the words, "who wrote it?"

"I did."

"I see." I know what's coming.

"And I'm also producing and directing."

I feel my throat constricting. My stomach feels cold. I'd like to shout, 'RUN WHILE YOU STILL HAVE THE CHANCE!,' but that would be grounds for dismissal.

"Do you have a performance schedule?"

"Not yet."

"How large is the house?"

"We may remove a few rows to accommodate the set, so I'm not sure yet."

"Do you want reserved seats or general admission?"

"What's general admission?"

I suppress the urge to tell him that no one will be admitted unless accompanied by a five-star general. "That means that you don't get a specific seat when you buy a ticket, but can sit anywhere that someone else is not sitting."

"Huh?"

"In other words, first come, first served."

"What?"

The jerk still doesn't get it. "Like a movie."

"Oh, I see. Like a movie."

"Reserved seating or general admission?"

"I'm not sure yet, let me think about it."

Great. "How much are you charging?"

"I don't know. What's the average price for the shows you handle?"

"Well, that depends. Some of our shows are ten dollars, some are six, some are twenty-five. It depends on the cost of the production."

"Hmm, let's say fifteen."

"Great," I say, finally getting some definite information. "When do you want the tickets to go on sale?"

"Tomorrow."

"But, sir . . . Mr. Bly, we have to get them printed first."

"Gee, you know I didn't think of that."

And so it goes. I deal with fools like this all the time and I sometimes feel like warning them that they're getting themselves into something that they can't begin to understand without some prior experience. When their shows finally open and play to an empty theater night after night, they come around looking for sympathy. If they ever came right out and asked, I'd suggest that they'd probably be better off driving a cab. But they never ask for my opinion and I just keep my mouth shut because I hate job hunting.

*

When Donald called and told me that the date had been set for his first one-man show, I was probably just as happy about it as he was.

"And that's not all," he said, "I've got a new boyfriend. Let's have dinner Tuesday night and we'll talk."

"Great, where?"

"I just discovered this wonderful place that serves Vietnamese cuisine."

"You're joking."

"No, it's real and it's terrific."

It was a small place at the edge of Soho, run by a Vietnamese family. The decor was very simple, almost austere, with white tablecloths, cane-backed chairs, and walls bedecked with photos of rice paddies. The lighting was a bit bright for my taste, but the place was clean, the waiter friendly, and it was so quiet we could talk without screaming at each other.

Donald ordered for both of us. The first course consisted of scallions wrapped in some kind of flaky dough, that we dipped in a tangy sauce. Very tasty.

"The show starts December 10th and runs for two weeks. At the Horse's Mouth Gallery on Prince Street."

I chomped on my scallions-in-a-blanket.

"The first painting will be one I did of you in your apartment."

"I can't believe it. I'm gonna be an objet d'art!"

"I was thinking maybe you could get the galleries editor of the *Clarion* to review the show."

"No problem. He owes me a favor since I wrote nice things about his lover's cabaret act. So tell me about Mr. Right. Where'd you meet him?"

"At the Met."

"No."

"Yes. I noticed him cruising me between the first and second acts of *La Traviata*. When it was over, we sort of gravitated toward each other in the lobby. We swapped phone numbers, had a few dates, and the next thing I knew we were referring to each other as boyfriends."

"How romantic."

Just then the waiter appeared with the second course. Thin slices of raw beef which we were to submerge in a small chafing dish of boiling oil.

"One second for rare," instructed Donald, "three seconds for medium, and seven seconds for burnt."

My first attempt was too well-done, but after that I cooked each slice to perfection. "What's his name?"

"Lorenzo."

"Is he cute?"

"I'll say. Half Italian and half Puerto Rican. Very sexy."

"Wow, sounds like a potent combination."

"He's beautiful. A graduate student of N.Y.U. Russian department. Literature."

I raised my cup of green tea. "To your show, and to Lorenzo."

Dessert was a platter of semi-sweet rice cakes that dissolved on the tongue like cotton candy.

We departed, strolled back to Sheridan Square, and had a few celebratory cocktails at the Corral.

──── Chapter Nine ────

It's impossible to leave my apartment — at any time, on any day — without getting hundreds of requests for spare change. From the sidewalk just outside of my building to the subway entrance on the corner, there is a gauntlet of winos with mottled skin and stringy hair, dressed in shabby clothes. Hands outstretched, faces in supplication, they are unavoidable. I usually walk past, trying to ignore them. Some are downright nasty and curse me when I don't dip into my pocket, others are polite and wish me a pleasant day in spite of my lack of generosity.

I always feel bad about not contributing to their alcohol budget, but I simply can't afford to. I earn barely enough to keep my own life intact and were I to give a quarter to even half of those who ask, I'd soon be out on the street and in competition with the ones who've already staked out their territory. And competition is just what they don't need. There are only so many corners available for franchise in this city.

I make my way to the subway and standing right by the token booth is another group who expect everyone to give them their change. Once the train arrives and I'm sitting and reading a book, men — in some strange religious garb — prowl the aisles soliciting contributions. I do my best to pretend they are invisible and dive deeper into whatever text I'm reading. Reaching Times Square, I race to get to the box office on time only to be confronted with another horde of panhandlers — these far more aggressive than their counterparts in Sheridan Square.

I can usually fight off the guilt, but it's a daily battle. The people who make me feel bad at work — simply for doing my job properly — stalk the guilt-area of my consciousness like patrolmen. And the beggars who demand money cause me to wonder what my life would be like if I were out on the street hustling quarters.

I don't think that I'm a monster and get angry when people make me out to be one of the evil ones.

Mike is my only source of comfort. "Those jerks asking for money on the street probably make more per hour than we do," he says.

And, aside from the legitimately homeless and destitute, he's probably right. Not only that, but they don't even have to file any income tax forms. I've always heard rumors that the beggars in any city are well organized and make themselves appear to be more miserable to inspire the sympathy of suckers. When their working day is done, they go home to nicely furnished rooms to count up their booty. How can one separate the charlatans from the genuinely destitute and the homeless? It's a mystery to me. I wonder if the dishonest ones ever feel guilty about separating people from their hard-earned incomes? If they experience any emotional qualms about the nature of their work, then I guess we are on equal terms. If they do not, then I have been unduly stigmatized. I hope their guilt tortures their sense of fair play as my conscience chastises me for ignoring their requests.

*

One night, after Amos had been living with me for over a month, Donald and I went to the Anvil. I supposed Amos was at work, but there he was, dancing with someone who was a stranger to me. He saw us on the fringe of the dance floor and brought his friend over.

"This is my partner at the restaurant — Sandy."

We shook hands and the four of us danced for a while. Sandy was tall and had shaggy black hair. Slightly overweight and affable, he impressed me as an easy-going, nice person. When we left the dance floor, he bought us all drinks and it didn't occur to me at the time that this was a foolish thing to do if one was a waiter and not earning much in tips.

I remembered this when I met Sandy on the street about a week later. I was passing by the dry cleaner right around the corner from my apartment and Sandy was smoking a cigarette, sitting on a car parked at the curb.

"Sandy, right?"

"Yes. You're Amos' lover."

"When it's convenient for him. How are things going?"

"Just great," he said, "couldn't be better."

"I understand it's been kind of slow at the restaurant."

"Are you kidding? It's never been better. I've been clearing over a hundred in tips every night."

My jaw almost hit the sidewalk. "Amos too?"

"Of course. How else do you think he could afford to score all the coke."

My senses snapped to attention and I played dumb. "Yeah, wonderful coke."

"You're so lucky to have Amos," he said. "He's such a generous guy. He gets me loaded almost every night."

"Yeah, generous guy."

I told Sandy I'd see him around, turned the corner, and climbed the stairs to the apartment. I sat down and cried. Every incidence of my foolishness paraded through my memory, yet I could not find an instance in which I'd been made to feel more stupid. I was paying Amos' bills and he was buying cocaine, by the truckload apparently, and not only had I not seen one grain of it, I'd not had the slightest notion of what was happening.

The tears kept coming. My stomach tightened and my brain felt like a mass of hot coals. I decided to ask Amos to move out the next time I saw him. But I had no idea when that would be.

*

When my review of the Meg Christian concert appeared in the *Clarion,* I had it xeroxed and sent a copy to almost everyone I knew. I felt that a new life was starting for me and I thought about spending the rest of my existence behind a typewriter instead of a microphone. It was an appealing vision. Rather than having to perform four or five sets a night and drag myself home at four in the morning; rather than spending all my income — after the bills were paid — on rehearsal studios, demo tapes, and taxis to transport my equipment to the clubs, I could simply buy a ream of paper, sit down, and write. No more having to rely on musicians who are never on time, no more dealing with dishonest club owners or snotty would-be rock stars.

My fee for the review was only fifteen dollars and I didn't get it until six months later. Still, I was content. I'd always wanted to be a writer, even though I'd never done anything about it. I figured if I was capable of writing five paragraphs about a performance, I could just as easily write the first five paragraphs of a short story. Or a novel. But I knew that I had a lot to learn about the world of writing, editing, and publishing. So I phoned the paper and asked the editor if I could do more. He was enthusiastic.

"What we want to do is cover musical events by openly gay musicians. But if there's nothing gay happening that week, you can write about any music performance you want."

"That sounds great," I said. "What's coming up?"

"There's nothing that I know of for a few weeks. The first week of April there's a concert by the New York City Gay Men's Chorus. We'll want a piece on that. If you want to do anything else before that, just let me know."

It was the perfect opportunity for me. Between my experience as a performer with folk, rock, and country, my jazz education in Boston and my lessons in classical music at the record store, I had an unusually diverse background. I felt that I could write about any aspect of music. This I set out to prove. In the first six months of my new career I reviewed a jazz-rock band, an environmentalist folk singer, a torchy cabaret artist, a handful of country albums, a Stevie Wonder concert, a harpsichord recital, and the aforementioned Meg Christian and Gay Men's Chorus.

The editor phoned one day, about a year after I'd started writing for him.

"I was wondering if you'd be interested in becoming our music editor? It doesn't pay yet, but as the circulation picks up, you'll eventually receive a small salary."

I accepted the offer, finished my performing obligations, and refused any subsequent bookings.

*

I was passing a bookstore and saw a trade paperback in the window titled *The Queens of Country Music.* I decided to pick it up as a gift for Max. When I arrived at the Charm School, it reeked of patchouli. Wearing a Marie Antoinette wig and frilly gown, Max looked like a hybrid of plantation belle and bordello Jezebel.

"Howdy," he drawled as I entered.

He led me down the hall and as we entered the living room, I handed him the book. He read the title to himself, then lifted his eyes. "Sugar, *I'm* the queen of country music and don't you forget it!" Turning to the contents, his finger followed the list of names. "Patsy, Loretty, Tammy, Dolly, they do okay for white women. But this Babs Mandrell, I don't know about her. She's too squeaky clean to be real. You know? She must be hiding something fierce."

He offered me some coke 'n' toke which I was happy to accept and then he switched on a tape. He lip-synched

Patsy, Loretta, Tammy, and Dolly perfectly, swiveling his hips, sculpting the air with his hands.

"Not bad," I said, "for a black woman."

"Listen to you," he said. "The next step is to really learn how to sing like this."

"Then what?"

"Go to Nashville and become a star. I'll be the first black lady to make a country record."

I shook my head. "Not true. What about 'Fairytale' by the Pointer Sisters? A lot of black ladies have cut country material."

"Oh yeah? The exception that proves the rule. Name three others."

"Candi Staton, Ann Peebles, and Millie Jackson."

"No shit?"

"No shit."

"And there are more?" he asked, scarcely believing.

"Aretha Franklin, Gladys Knight, and Diana Ross."

"You're putting me on."

"Nope. I'll make you a tape."

"I'm gonna get me a guitar and learn to play it."

"Max—"

"Max*ine*."

"Maxine, I'm sure you can do whatever you set your mind to do."

"Thanks for the vote of confidence, sugar. Pass me that joint."

*

I can picture the Aliens who have been dispatched to study three American cities, when they convene to compare notes. They are in human disguise, sitting around a large table in the conference room of their starship.

The first Alien hands around snapshots of New Orleans and begins to speak. "The city of New Orleans is on the Mississippi River and has many nice buildings and flowers. The humans take their time moving about and everyone drinks large quantities of an inebriant called liquor that comes in different colors and flavors. Recreational sex — that which does not have to do with procreation — is a favorite pastime and once a year the inhabitants celebrate an old holiday in which everyone dresses up in garish costumes and carouses all day and night. It is a very musical city and almost every form of American music flourishes in the bars, clubs, and concert halls. The city has much charm and it is worth further investigation."

The second Alien rises and slips a cassette into a VCR. "The city of Boston is composed mainly of students and teachers and you cannot go very far without encountering a school of some kind. The educational resources range from large universities of higher learning to schools for secretaries, bartenders, and automobile mechanics. Lovely parks are laid out everywhere and on sunny afternoons it is not unusual to see the students reading their books out-of-doors. Some are very serious about their studies while others are more concerned with taking illegal drugs and playing a game called frisbee. This game is unlike any other we have observed. Boston is most certainly ripe for more intensive study."

The third Alien, its head bandaged and its arm in a sling, speaks with a trembling voice. "I had intended to show you photographs of New York City but an Earthling stole my camera. About half the city consists of modern architecture built in the last fifty years and scheduled for dilapidation in about another ten. The other part is where the poor live and their buildings should have been leveled years ago but are in a state of slow rot. The humans are always in a hurry and move about as though being chased. During the course of my week there, I was stuck on an underground train for several hours, held up with a lethal weapon pointed at my head, beaten by a gang of male adolescents wielding baseball bats — a device invented for use in a game played by adults who refuse to grow up — and asked for charitable contributions wherever I went. The city has many concert halls, museums, and libraries, but most of the humans stay at home and watch video screens or go to dance halls where the loud music eventually makes them deaf. New York City merits extensive observation but I recommend that future investigators go in teams, undercover, and heavily armed."

The first two Aliens reapply for more terms of Earth study. The third requests an extended vacation.

*

When I finally met Lorenzo — at Donald's railroad flat on Sullivan Street — I had to agree that Donald had met a rare individual. His midnight hair, bright green eyes flecked with gold, bronze skin, and well-muscled body did not impress me nearly as much as his polite manner, quick mind, and friendly air. I don't know if he worked at being so agreeable or if it was completely natural, but he was the kind of person for whom I felt an immediate affinity. We shook hands and sat at Donald's butcher-block kitchen table, nibbling paté with Dijon and Italian bread, sipping Chablis. Paintings and sketches covered almost all of the wall space. The music of Philip Glass played softly in the background.

"Donald tells me you study Russian literature."

"True. I've been interested in all things Russian ever since I was young, but I don't quite know why."

"Must've been those Rachmaninoff piano concertos," said Donald, grinning.

"Actually," said Lorenzo, spreading mustard on a small piece of bread, "the first Russian music that got to me was *The Rite Of Spring*. But when I read Turgenev's *First Love*, my fate was sealed."

"I love that one too," I said. "That and *Anna Karenina* are my favorite Russian novels."

"Ah, among my favorites as well." He glanced at Donald. "Loverman here won't read anything that wasn't written in English."

"I don't trust translations."

I looked at Donald in amazement. "What? Since when? What about all the Andre Gide you've read?"

"Well," said Donald, "I used to read a lot of translations. But not anymore."

"Go on," said Lorenzo.

"I recently finished reading three different translations of Baudelaire's *Les Fleurs Du Mal*. And they were all different! I didn't know which one comes closest to the original. It suddenly dawned on me that reading a translation can never be like reading the original. So if I were to read something by, say, Flaubert, I wouldn't be getting it from the source, but someone else's *interpretation* of not only Flaubert, but French and English too."

"That's true," I said as Lorenzo shook his head in agreement. "So, does that mean you won't read anything that wasn't written originally in English?"

"That's right," But I'm going to study French so I can read all of Gide in the original—and then, Lorenzo's going to teach me Russian."

"I am?"

"You are."

They appeared to be acknowledging some private joke.

Lorenzo smiled at Donald, then looked at me. "Donald says that you read a lot."

"Yes," I confessed, "I'm a print junkie. I'll read anything that I haven't already read."

"I admire your adventurousness," said Lorenzo. "I keep rereading the same books that I know I'll like. Unless I have to read something for class. I guess I'm afraid to try something that may not satisfy. What are you reading now?"

"Henry James' *The Golden Bowl*. Can you believe that I made it through the American Educational Mind Processor and never read Henry James? I'm probably the last person on Earth to get around to him."

"I haven't read him yet," said Donald.

"Nor I," said Lorenzo.

"Well, as soon as I'm finished, it's yours to fight over. I love it so far."

"Donald said you're an expert on gay literature."

"I wouldn't call myself an expert. But ever since I started writing for the *Clarion*, I began to read the book reviews and found out about all of this stuff I never knew existed: novels, stories, and poems by gay writers about gay people written for gay readers. There's tons. I'm slowly making my way through it."

The talk turned to the state of gay liberation and the subject of AIDS — something we were just becoming aware of.

"It's only happening to gay guys who are super promiscuous," said Donald.

"I thought it was happening to guys who do a lot of drugs," I said.

"I have a scary feeling it's going to get a lot worse before it gets any better," said Lorenzo.

*

Jennifer called last night, breathless with excitement. "I got the part!"

"Which part?"

"Susan Vandermeer, bitch queen of *Hamilton Heights*."

"You're going to be a TV star," I said, amazed.

"Daytime, anyway. But the money's incredible, the part's easy, and I can live with the taping schedule."

"What does Magda think?"

"She still thinks the television is something to throw her cereal at."

"Smart kid."

"That she is."

"When do I get to babysit again?"

"Anytime."

"Have you heard from Larry?"

"I called him to tell him I got the part. He accused me of selling out. I, of course, told him to go to hell."

107

"Is he still offering financial support?"

"Yes, and I'm still refusing."

"Jennifer, sometimes you're a mystery. Why?"

"Because I want Magda for myself and my future husband if I ever meet him. Larry thinks that if he sends me money, he owns me and can tell me what to do."

"Have a heart. He'd probably feel better if you'd let him send you some money."

"But then I'd be indebted to him."

"No, you wouldn't."

"Yes, I would. When I think that he was all set to arrange an abortion, I could scream. When I think that I even considered it, I could die. How would you feel knowing that you'd prevented a beautiful child like Magda from being born?"

"Don't tell me you think abortion should be thrown back into the dark ages again?"

"Not at all. I think every woman should have the choice. I wanted my baby and I made my decision. That's not to say that if I ever got pregnant again and decided that I didn't want the baby that I'd have it anyway. It's a woman's right to decide these things and men should have nothing to do with it."

I wasn't sure if I agreed with her — about men having nothing to do with it. But it was her body, her child, and her life so I didn't argue the point.

*

Mike and I had another fight. We wound up not speaking to each other for two days. And when we reconciled, we couldn't even remember what the argument had been about.

I recall that we were both pretty wired from our crazy schedules. It was late at night, exhaustion had a tight grip on us, and we disagreed about something that must have been pretty trivial. I guess we subconsciously realized that whatever it was, it wasn't worth fighting over, so we simply stopped talking.

The silence lasted too long for me. I missed the "good nights," "good mornings," and "how was your days?" And sleeping in the same bed with someone you are not talking to can be rather unrestful. But we made up, kissed, and hugged. Everything is all right now.

Given the choice between Amos' binges of absence and Mike's silent treatment, I'd rather have my lover here and angry than away and completely indifferent.

—— Chapter Ten ——

Although Mike isn't officially living here yet, he spends about four or five nights a week with me. We decided to allow his roommate two months to find a replacement so he won't be burdened with the entire rent bill. Meanwhile, Mike is slowly moving his stuff in and I'm still sorting through all the stacks of press releases, newspapers, and magazines, trying to determine what to discard.

It's cold enough now to keep the windows closed most of the time and this cuts down on the amount of street noise entering the apartment. Now we can listen to softer, less thickly textured music — like unaccompanied traditional singers — without too much distraction. Also, the quiet passages of symphonies and sonatas are not intruded upon as much.

The various contingents of the Earthling parade, as viewed from my window, are starting to bundle up for the colder weather and even the hardiest have packed away their fall wardrobes and are wearing scarves and gloves. The fashions of autumn, as striking sometimes as the richly hued foliage, are fading and with the leaves already starting to fall, it won't be long before everyone looks as drab as a naked, leafless tree.

After I found out that Amos was all too capable of deception, my attitude toward him changed drastically. I found myself losing interest and began to think of a way that I could get rid of him without making myself the bad guy. Although he had been more than willing to forsake New Orleans and move here, I felt guilty about asking someone to move out after so vehemently encouraging him to move in.

And everything was complicated by his brother and sister-in-law. It had reached a point where Matthew and Gloria phoned regularly. If Amos was not at home — which was often — I would chat with them. And they, unwittingly, clued me to Amos' history of bad habits and reprehensible behavior. I thought I was to blame for his being so irresponsible.

Matthew called one day and, after asking me how I was, asked to speak to Amos.

"He's not here."

"Do you know where he is?"

It was ten o'clock in the morning so I couldn't say he was at work. I decided not to cover for him this time. I was tired of lying.

"No, I don't."

"Will you have him call me when he gets in?"

"Of course."

"You know, I've been meaning to tell you how happy Gloria and I are that he's finally settling down. He used to get into all kinds of trouble and it seems that these past few months he's been living with you, he's turned over a new leaf. If I told you how many times he used to disappear for days, get too stoned to find his way back home, or have to get bailed out, you wouldn't believe it."

I didn't say a word, which required a great deal of self-restraint.

"Can you guys come to dinner a week from Friday night?"

"If Amos doesn't have to work, we'd love to."

I made a note of the date and assured Matthew that I'd mention it to Amos and have him call.

I had too much on my mind to ponder Amos' shady past. I was still working two jobs and performing on weekends. The gigs were going well—the sound engineer taped them all for me and I'd study the tapes to assess my progress. Listening to earlier tapes back-to-back with the later ones showed tremendous improvement in my pitch, tempos, and instrumental accompaniment. It had become too expensive to hire musicians and taxi equipment around town, so I was performing solo. And though I was pleased with the songs I was writing, it was difficult to attract a larger audience. I had my small cult who always came to listen, but finding new ways to increase my following was not easy and involved further expense. Advertising was out of the question. And Amos' spendthrift ways were practically making me bankrupt. I didn't know what to do. But I knew sooner or later something would have to change.

Two days after Matthew called, the phone rang and it was Gloria. At first I thought she was going to chastise me because I still hadn't seen Amos, therefore he hadn't gotten the message and hadn't called them. But she never mentioned that.

"How are you today?"

"Just fine, how are you?" I asked, nervously.

"Good. Listen, we have a problem."

"Oh?" My palms began to sweat.

"Matthew and I were invited to a wedding Saturday night and originally we were going to leave Christopher with a friend of mine but she's just come down with the flu and probably won't be up and around until after the weekend." She paused dramatically. "So we were wondering if Christopher could stay with you guys Saturday night? We would drop him off in the afternoon, say around one o'clock, and pick him up the same time on Sunday. The wedding is in

Connecticut and we've been invited to stay the night. Of course, we could drive back that night, but we thought maybe you guys could handle it."

"Of course we can handle it," I said, meaning *I* could. I still couldn't work up the nerve to tell her that her brother-in-law was a complete fuck-up who couldn't be trusted with anything. "In fact, I'm flattered that you thought of us. It won't be a problem at all. I don't know if Amos has to work that night or not, but I'm not performing so at least one of us can be here. You go to the wedding, have a good time, and don't worry about a thing."

"Are you sure?"

"Sure I'm sure."

"It won't be an imposition?"

"Not at all, it'll be fun."

As soon as I got off the phone I called the club and canceled my gig, assuring the manager that I'd find a replacement. Then I called a singer/songwriter buddy who was happy to fill in.

It seemed like the perfect opportunity to explore my paternal feelings somewhat. Twenty-four hours with a youngster might help to indicate whether I had any aptitude for fatherhood. And chances were that Amos wouldn't be around so it would be a solo flight. I silently thanked Matthew and Gloria for trusting a gay man with their son and happily looked forward to my weekend with a six-year-old.

*

The second time I saw Lorenzo was at the Soho gallery where Donald's one-man show had just opened. Both of them were dressed in suits and ties. They looked very handsome. Until then I'd only seen Donald in jeans and plaid shirts. He kept running his finger around the inside of his collar, unused to such restricting attire. Or maybe he was just nervous about the show. Lorenzo looked so comfortable I automatically assumed he was used to dressing up. I wore my usual jeans and a plaid. At first I felt slightly out of place because there were a lot of people in formal wear. But there were enough people in street clothes, like me, so that the suits and ties, gowns and jewels were not too intimidating.

The gallery was on the second floor of an old building and the space had been divided into thirds, each room consisting of four white walls with an entranceway at one of the corners.

Donald's paintings — some of his normal-sized canvasses and some of his gigantic ones — were hung three or four to a wall. His bold strokes and bright colors filled the room. Walking in was like entering a huge kaleidoscope. My favorite paintings were a very large one — approximately eight feet by eight — very abstract with deep blues and a vibrant splash of orange, and a smaller, very colorful still life of his studio with coffee cans of brushes, several palettes, and tubes of paint.

After surveying the dozen or so paintings I approached the artist and his lover. Lorenzo handed me a glass of champagne.

"Congratulations." We clinked glasses and I kissed them both on the cheek. "You two look like peacocks." I winked at them and turning to Donald said, "The show looks great."

"I already sold two paintings," he said, beaming.

"That's wonderful. Which ones?"

"The big one over there," he pointed to the blue and orange canvas that had immediately seduced me "and the nature study over there," he pointed to an eerie forest scene.

But that was all the time they could spare me. Donald was beseiged by other artists and several poets who had come by. He introduced me to a few people whom I'd heard of, and I eventually got into an interesting conversation with a poet who was known primarily for his lush, rural descriptions and a sculptor who specialized in assemblages constructed of found objects. The talk centered, naturally, on the shrinking government subsidy for artists. "Where is Jimmy Carter now that we really need him?" joked the sculptor.

I left the show feeling elated for Donald and walked back to Sheridan Square in a contented frame of mind.

Two days after the show, when Donald called me, I was still glowing.

"You made me feel so proud! How does it feel to be a successful artiste?"

"The show isn't over yet. Still a week and a half to go."

"Wouldn't you consider it a success?"

"Definitely. But, as usual, there's good news and bad."

"Uh, oh," I said cautiously, "tell me the good news first."

"I sold two more paintings."

"That's great."

"And someone wanted to buy the study of you and your apartment, but I decided I wanted you to have it, so I quoted a totally outrageous figure."

"Have you gone crazy? You passed up a sale?"

"In the first place, I've already recouped my expenses. In the second place, I want you to have it."

"I'd love to have it, but you should have sold it. Or donated it to a museum or something. Who'll ever see it in my apartment?"

"That's not the point. It's yours. I'll have it framed and bring it over."

"I can't believe it, my own objet d'art. You shouldn't have, but thank you."

"Are you sitting down?"

"Yes."

"Can you handle some bad news?"

"How bad?"

"Bad enough."

"Okay. Shoot."

"Lorenzo has AIDS. The doctor says less than a year."

*

I still hadn't met Jennifer's new boyfriend, Larry — the computer programmer. Jen called one day about three months after she'd met him and asked if I'd like to meet her for dinner. We ate at a small, dark place just a few blocks from here that serves the best burgers in town.

"The rabbit died."

"What rabbit? I didn't even know that you had one or that it was sick."

"I'm pregnant, silly."

"You're kidding!"

"No, I'm in the family way."

"What are you going to do?"

"Have it."

"You? You're the least likely candidate for motherhood that I've ever known."

"I'm going through with it. Without Larry."

"Without Larry?"

"He wants me to get an abortion. No way."

"But you can't have a kid. You drink and smoke and do too many drugs."

"I quit."

"Just like that?"

"Haven't had a cigarette or a drink in three days and I threw out what was left of my grass and coke."

"Threw it out? You could've at least given it to me."

"I wanted it out of my apartment as soon as I got the results."

"I'm amazed."

"I am too," she sighed. "but it's what I want."

"And what about Larry?"

"What about him?"

"It's his kid too."

"Yes, but he doesn't have to carry it around for nine months and besides, he wants me to kill it. I won't."

"Have you discussed marriage?"

"I don't want to marry him and he doesn't want to marry me. Anyway, his company wants to transfer him to California and it looks like he's going."

"So you're going to have a baby — out of wedlock — and raise it all by yourself?"

"Bingo."

"You're crazy."

"You've always known that. Anyway, I won't be completely alone. My mom will help out, and I think I can count on some friends too."

"Like me?"

"Like you."

"What can I do?"

"I've decided on natural childbirth and was wondering if you'd help me through the Lamaze training and assist at the delivery?"

"Are you serious?"

"Never been seriouser. You're always bitching about those latent paternal feelings of yours. Here's your chance to roll up your sleeves and find out what a real father goes through."

"It sort of sounds exciting, but it's scary too."

"I know you can do it. Besides, you just might get a short story out of it."

"You really know how to hit me where it hurts. But I'm almost convinced."

"I picked up a few manuals on the Lamaze method and I thought you could read them and let me know if you're interested."

I took the manuals home and read them. It didn't take very long. I started to think about it.

The next afternoon I was sitting by the window, smoking a joint. Around the corner came a man, holding the hand of a little boy. As they came closer I could make out their matching t-shirts: 'Gay Daddy,' said the man's. 'Son of Gay Daddy,' said the boy's.

I thought about what it would be like to be present when a child was born. I realized I would probably never have this opportunity again.

I called Jennifer. "It's me. I'll do it. When can we get together and talk nitty-gritty?"

*

Donald called. He said he was eating and sleeping better. But he was still angry and upset. I can't say I blame him.

"We need more support. We have to crowbar famous people from their closets. It's the only way. Average Americans don't give a shit about anything until their favorite movie and pop stars align themselves with a cause." He paused. "Are you listening."

"I'm here."

"Gay is the last taboo. Celebrities will spill every detail about their marital or psychological problems, difficulties with drugs or booze. But if they're gay, they have opposite sex escorts so the public won't know they're gay. Can you figure it out?"

"No."

"It's okay to be a manic-depressive, wife-beating alcoholic, but falling in love with someone of the same sex is unmentionable."

"Crazy world."

"Gay stars think that if they tell the truth about their personal lives, sales of their records, posters, and videos will decline. That's nonsense! For every fan they might lose by coming out, they'd probably gain another five. We gays need our heroes and role models too."

"You don't have to sell me," I reminded him, "I'm on your side."

"But it's so absurd," he sighed.

"Well, what do you expect from a country that burns books, censors song lyrics, and says it's okay for kids to see people getting hacked apart with meat cleavers, but it's not okay for kids to see people making love."

"Maybe you're right. Maybe I'm expecting too much."

"No, you're not expecting too much. Just remember

what you're dealing with and don't expect miracles overnight."

"You're right. But ever since Lorenzo died, I feel like I should do something. We've got to beat this AIDS thing. It's too monstrous. Something must be done! I guess I've been in a rut lately. But now it's time to claw my way out and fight back!"

*

Mike and I had known each other for about a year, and had been living together for about four months when we celebrated our first Christmas and Hanukkah together. I think it was one of the most wonderful times I've ever known.

Mike—the Baptist—went out and bought a menorah and candles. I—the Jew—went shopping for a Christmas tree. We set it up next to the television and Mike unpacked all of his ornaments; a collection he'd been assembling for years. Bells, birds, crystals, globes, flashing lights, stars, and angels. I decorated the tree all by myself. Mike coached a little from the sidelines.

"Move the dove a few branches higher. Move that crystal off to the side. That's it."

I plugged in the lights and the tree came to life. As lovely as any I'd ever seen. We draped a bit of tinsel over several branches and our tree shimmered like a frosted wedding cake.

For seven nights we lit the menorah, which sat by the window on my typing table. I recited the Hebrew prayer for the Hanukkah lights phrase by phrase, with Mike echoing the strange language. His pronunciation of Hebrew was funny and charming. By the seventh night, he had the prayer memorized.

"With all of the candles burning, it looks so beautiful," he said.

With the tree all lit up and the candles all aglow, our apartment looked enchanted. For the first time in my life I felt the rapture that is supposed to accompany the holiday season. Until then it had been a yearly ritual devoid of feeling or meaning. With a lover to share the beauty and serenity, the holiday spirit moved me in a way that I'd not thought possible.

Chapter Eleven

Last night I had to rush Mike to the emergency ward of Beth Israel Hospital. Apparently he has some kind of tooth or gum infection. The day before yesterday when I got home from work, he complained about some sensitivity in his lower, left-hand jaw. I suggested that he make an appointment with the dental clinic. He refused, claiming the pain would subside. When I walked in last night after a wretched eight-hour shift at Ticket Pandemonium, he looked like he had a golf ball wedged between his teeth and cheek. When I asked how he was feeling, he started to moan and cry.

We took a taxi to the hospital and he was examined by a young dentist. A willowy black woman. She said that a tooth had to be extracted, but surgical procedures were required; something the emergency room is not equipped for. She gave him two prescriptions: one for the pain, another for the infection. We searched Manhattan up and down looking for an all-night pharmacy and finally found one at Lexington and 50th. It took longer to get the prescriptions filled than it had to wait for Mike to be examined.

When we arrived back at the apartment, the first thing I did was make a note to phone for a dental appointment. Mike took the pills and fell asleep about an hour later. I held him in my arms and recalled the night—about two months after we'd met—that he held me all night while I was freaking out over a friend who'd just died of AIDS. I was so upset I hadn't slept for two nights and by the third I was so tired and achy, I was weak and shaking. Mike massaged my back, neck, and shoulders, cradled me in his arms, and talked to me soothingly of unimportant things until I finally fell asleep.

*

The office of the *Clarion* was right below Canal Street in a refurbished industrial loft. Exposed pipes and beams dominated the walls and ceiling. Typewriters, typesetting machines, copiers, and drafting tables occupied most of the cluttered floor space. The rest was taken up by stacks of out-of-print books and back copies of various gay newspapers and magazines.

Published by a small corporation that was also responsible for a cock-shot magazine and a literary journal, all three periodicals were produced by the same team of editors, typesetters, and art directors. The only thing different was the writers. The *Clarion* was staffed by writers who were either political analysts or arts critics. *Man to Man* consisted mostly of pictorials featuring naked hustlers simulating sex. Writers were, therefore, unnecessary. The contents of *Lavender Lane*, the literary journal, was comprised of five columns, all written by the publisher's friends who shared his point of view and taste. Or lack thereof.

When I began writing occasional reviews for the *Clarion*, I spent very little time at the office. All of my writing was done at home and I'd simply drop off my reviews and leave. But when I became music editor, I'd spend a few hours a week at the office line-editing the other music critic's reviews. Eventually I got to know the editor.

His name was Lee and he was a brilliant political writer. Slim and cute, he wore glasses and had golden brown hair that was long and straight. He was largely unconcerned with the arts coverage, so the music section of the paper was entirely my responsibility. Lee and I got along splendidly because I didn't care about politics and he was equally indifferent to music. It was a perfect relationship.

The publisher, however, could not tolerate any music that wasn't from an opera or Broadway show and believed — in his small-minded way — that gay men only listened to Verdi and Sondheim. I made sure that rock, folk, reggae, soul, jazz, country, disco, and chamber music were given regular coverage which did not please the publisher, but drew quite a positive response from the paper's readers.

At first I was worried about the potential friction, but he wound up giving me free reign. After all, he couldn't really fire me because I was not getting paid and was, therefore, a volunteer rather than an employee. There was no line of eager music editors waiting for the job, and why dismiss someone who's willing to do so much work for no money? The payment, for me, was the opportunity to learn the behind-the-scenes stuff about writing, editing, and publishing. No school could have provided a better education.

*

I don't know if Jennifer and Russell will ever live together or marry, but they make a terrific couple. He has no trouble dealing with the fact that she has a daughter from a previous relationship and seems to dote on Magda as much as I do. He says that he doesn't get along well with Jennifer's mother, but none of her boyfriends have ever earned her approval as she is, according to Jennifer, always suspicious of her daughter's lovers. I wonder if Jennifer will be as protective of Magda as her mother is of her. Some people break out of these cycles. Others perpetuate them.

The only problem I can foresee that might possibly get in the way of Jennifer and Russell is their careers. They are both ambitious and competitive. When things are going well for him and not for her, she broods about it. Apparently he weathers the bad times with more tranquility. Actresses and musicians have a lot in common as far as career struggles go.

As long as both of them can keep working regularly, everything should be fairly smooth and easy. If any two people I
know have a chance of sustaining a long-term relationship,
they do. But a wedding ceremony would surprise me completely.

*

It was a breezy, sun-filled day and though I was used
to spending my Saturdays preparing for five sets of performances, I enjoyed taking some time off. I read for a while,
listened to some music, then went for a walk to the pier. The
streets were packed with natives and tourists, all enjoying the
promise of spring.

I arrived home at about 12:30 and at 1:05, Matthew,
Gloria, and Christopher appeared at the door. Matthew car-
ried a small suitcase, Gloria, a casserole she'd prepared, and
Christopher clutched a shopping bag full of his toys.

"Where's Amos?" asked Matthew.

"He's doing a double shift today — lunch and dinner. He
won't be home until after midnight," I lied. I hadn't heard
from him for four days and knew he could be anywhere from
the Club Baths on the Lower East Side to the beach at Key
West.

"Are you sure you can handle this?" asked Gloria.

"Of course. Don't worry about a thing. Just enjoy your
trip to Connecticut and the wedding."

Gloria handed me a slip of paper. "Here's the number
should you have to get in touch."

"Okay."

"Don't hesitate to phone if the need should arise."

"I promise, I'll call if I have to."

Gloria kissed my cheek. "You're a darling."

Then she hugged Christopher and said, "You be a good
little man. Don't give your uncles any trouble."

He nodded and I whisked his parents out the door
before he could think about it and start crying. I told him

to sit down and asked if he wanted anything to drink. He shook his head.

"Would you like to play with your toys, watch television, or go for a walk?"

He shook his head again.

I placed the casserole in the refrigerator, took his suitcase into the bedroom, and sat beside him on the couch. He was wearing a Hulk Hogan t-shirt, jeans, and saddle shoes.

"I didn't know you were a wrestling fan," I said, pointing to the cartoon image on his shirt.

"Daddy and me always watch it every Saturday morning. But we didn't today because we had to pack."

"Would you like to watch it tonight?"

His eyes widened. "It's on tonight?" He could hardly believe it.

"Yes."

"What time?"

"Midnight."

"I'm not allowed to stay up that late."

"Well, if you want to, you can."

"Really?"

"Really."

"Wow." He opened his bag of toys and pulled out a Hulk Hogan doll. Then an Iron Sheik doll. "Kabowie!" he shrieked, throwing the Sheik on the floor. He pinned it with the Hulk Hogan doll, counted to three and raised the Hulk doll triumphantly. "Hulk Hogan, still world's champ!"

I chuckled. "Are you hungry?"

"No."

"Do you want to play with your toys?"

He nodded.

"Can I play too, or should I go into the bedroom and read?"

"I like to play by myself sometimes," he said. I couldn't believe how tactful he was. Surely I didn't have that kind of savvy when I was only six.

I brought my book into the bedroom and plopped stomach-down on the bed. Next door I could hear Hulk Hogan beating the shit out of the Iron Sheik. In this way, the afternoon slowly slipped away.

At about five o'clock I found Christopher sitting by the window looking down at Sheridan Square.

"Would you like to go out?"

"There's too many people."

"What time do you usually have dinner?"

"Six o'clock on the nose."

"Would you like to eat here or at a restaurant?"

"Can we have pizza?"

"Anything you want."

He clapped his hands. "Good. Mom never lets me have pizza for dinner."

"Well, your Mom and Dad are having fun at the wedding, so you can have fun too. Okay?"

He smiled and I tousled his hair.

"Mom hates it when people touch my hair."

"How do you feel about it?"

He thought for a moment. "It depends on the person."

"You're a smart young man," I said as his attention returned to the street below.

At six I pulled a sweater from his suitcase and helped him into it. We walked to Antonio's Pizza Cafe on Seventh Avenue. I ordered a large pie with everything but anchovies. He had a root beer, I sipped red wine. His manners astonished me; he placed his napkin on his lap before I had to tell him to and thanked the waitress when she served him his drink.

When we arrived home I turned on the television and he was surprised to learn that I didn't have a cable hookup. "We always watch movies after dinner on Saturday night. Until the babysitter comes and my parents go out."

"I don't have cable, but you can choose between *I Love Lucy* or *The Jeffersons*." Everything else looked pretty awful.

"What's *I Love Lucy?*"

"It's an old TV show that was a big hit when I was your age."

He decided on *The Jeffersons.* After that we watched *Archie Bunker's Place*, then *Gimme A Break.* Halfway into *Facts Of Life*, he was sleeping soundly. I carried him to the bed, stripped him to his underwear, and tucked him in.

*

An undisguised Alien could probably stroll through Sheridan Square without attracting a second glance. The cast of characters on the street — at any given time — is so diverse, the range so vast, the only ones who truly stand out are the tourists. The tourists from Earth, anyway. Between the New Wave kids with their outrageously dyed hair, the S&M guys in black leather and studs who call each other 'Mary,' the artistic types in faded work shirts and jeans, and the bag ladies and winos, the only obvious oddity is the visiting family on vacation.

Mama wears a salmon-colored pantsuit and a kerchief around her much-sprayed hair. Papa is dressed in a camel-tan leisure suit. Brother wears a hooded, red sweatshirt, tight jeans, bomber jacket, and white running shoes. Sister is clad in her boyfriend's varsity jacket, plaid skirt, and knee socks. A three-headed, four-armed Alien with purple skin and hair like eelgrass could waltz by and the only thing to attract the attention of a native West Villager would be the family of Earthling tourists.

"What's that?" asks Sister, pointing to a stoned punk.

"Probably a rock star," says Mama.

"What's that?" asks Sister, pointing to a group of leathermen.

"Probably a motorcycle club, like the Hell's Angels," says Papa.

"Get real, Dad," says Brother, "it's a bunch of gay guys cruising for sex."

Mama clucks her tongue. "Our son has such a wild imagination!"

"What's that?" asks Sister, pointing to the Alien.

"Now that's a homosexual," says Papa.

"Do you think he knows Joan Rivers?" asks Mama.

"Could be," says Papa. "Let's go back to the hotel."

They hail a taxi, disappear from the scene, and everything in Sheridan Square returns to normal.

*

At first, Lorenzo refused to accept the prognosis that predicted sudden death. But as the mortality rate climbed and AIDS became a hot news item, he finally came to accept the painful reality. And he decided not to fight it. Donald begged him to try chemotherapy, but Lorenzo refused because he'd seen pictures of patients whose skin was sallow and whose hair had begun to fall out. He elected to stay home most of the time and watch television. Donald would visit and try to cheer him up, but his despondency would not be broken. Eventually, he asked Donald not to visit anymore.

I called him a few times, but he always said — politely — that he was too tired to talk. I sent him several gay novels and he responded with a brief note of thanks. Donald was terribly upset at being shut out and called me constantly to try and alleviate his bitterness. I consoled him as best I could.

When Lorenzo entered the hospital with an advanced case of pneumonia, he allowed no visitors. He prepared a will in which he left all of his books and records to Donald and stipulated that there be no funeral ceremony. He asked that his family hold a private burial.

Uninvited, Donald attended the burial. He reported that out of Lorenzo's enormous family, only a sister, an aunt, and an uncle bothered to show up. "The rest of 'em were probably afraid of catching AIDS," he snickered.

"You can't get AIDS from a corpse," I said.

"Unless you have sex with it," he countered.

I knew that he was afraid that he had contracted the disease. That is the fear that every gay man has. Especially the ones whose lovers have died from it.

*

I began to read about natural childbirth. And with mild trepidation, looked forward to witnessing it. There would be lots of training, I knew, and doctors and nurses would be present when the time came, so I wasn't worried about the biological aspects.

But Jennifer's state of mind and attitude were extremely important. And I was, for all intents and purposes, the surrogate husband whose job it was to keep her in a positive frame of mind. We began spending more time together than we ever had before; strolling through Central Park on sunny afternoons, going to movies and concerts in the evenings. One night I prepared a light dinner for her at my apartment and afterwards, read poetry to her for the remainder of the evening. Larry had moved to Los Angeles and she had not yet met Russell. She'd put her career on hold after appearing as Amelia in an off-Broadway revival of *Othello* that had enjoyed a three-month run.

Our Lamaze training sessions took place on Wednesday nights. We began about four months into the pregnancy. Jennifer's hair was shorter than I'd ever seen it and she began to wear skirts more often. I didn't see her in a pair of jeans until several months after Magda was born.

The sessions took place in the office of Dr. Gilbert, a woman in her forties who didn't try to hide the streaks of gray in her hair. There were four couples apart from Jennifer and myself: Ted and Johanna, both upwardly mobile professionals in their late twenties; Susan and Fred — a white woman and black man who were always chuckling over some private joke; Bill and Marie — an older couple who already had two kids and were trying the natural method for the first time; and Linda and Ruth, a veterinarian and a librarian, who both had short, spiky hair and always wore black sweatshirts and jeans.

Everyone assumed I was the father of Jennifer's child-to-be, even though she made it clear that she was not married.

The first session was basically a lecture in which Dr. Gilbert told us about the importance of sharing our feelings and the need for mutual support. Both the mother and the coach can become prone to periods of fear or distrust — she warned us — and the psychological problems were the main thing to try to avoid.

The second session consisted of a demonstration of breathing techniques which all of us were expected to learn.

"Piece of cake," said Jennifer, inhaling short, fast breaths.

"Nothing to it," I agreed, doing the same.

For the third session, I arrived a bit early and sat next to Ruth, Linda's coach.

"You and I are the only ones who don't seem to be too nervous about all this," she said.

"I am pretty nervous," I confessed, "but I don't want Jennifer to know. I'm not the child's father."

"Who is?"

"Her ex-boyfriend."

"And you're her new boyfriend, how sweet."

"Actually," I said, clearing my throat, "we're just good friends. I'm gay," I added, so she'd understand.

"I am too," she said casually, "and so is Linda."

I almost asked for the lowdown on how Linda became pregnant, but decided against it.

"You're probably wondering why two lesbians would want to have a child."

"I'm sure you have excellent reasons," I said.

"This is between you and me," she said, lowering her voice.

"Of course."

"Linda was raped," she paused, "and decided against abortion. Besides, we always talked about raising a child. We could do just as good a job — if not better — than the straight couples we know."

"How is Linda dealing with the fact that she was raped?" I couldn't help asking.

"The memory haunts her sometimes and she'll start to cry. But she's a strong woman. Actually, she's doing very well, considering."

After the session I told Jennifer that Ruth and Linda were lovers, but I left out the part about the rape. I didn't want her to worry any more than she already had to.

*

I still haven't heard from the publisher who has my short story manuscript, but I've just had my third story published in a small press literary magazine.

I can't begin to describe the exhilaration I felt when it arrived in the mail. The editor put my name and the title of the story on the cover, and it's the first one you come to. The lead piece, as they say in publishing circles.

I called up everyone I knew and told them about it, then went out to make a tour of all the bookstores which stock the magazine. It was such a thrill to see my name on the same shelf with the names of others writers who are better known than I am. And some who I respect so much, I never would have believed that my name would ever be juxtaposed with theirs.

I have to keep reminding myself that the summit is still quite a ways off and that I've only begun to conquer the mountain. Still, the little signs of progress make the peak look like it's not quite as far away as it sometimes appears. But the top of the mountain seems impossible to reach while you're on the way up. Passing over in a plane is the only time it looks any less intimidating.

My goal is to become a full-time writer and be able to quit the box office. Not an easy thing these days unless you want to write exercise manuals, cat humor, or celebrity biographies. Writers of serious fiction and poetry have a tough time of it, but still persist. Few of us ever make it, but the ones who do give hope to all the others. Right now I'm an unsuccessful hopeful. Perhaps someday I'll be a success, an inspiration to others.

—— Chapter Twelve ——

Certain that Christopher was sleeping comfortably, I went back into the living room, turned off the television set, and picked up my book. I can't recall exactly which one it was, but it's safe to assume it was by an author whom I'd heard about but had not yet read.

I spent the rest of the evening reading, then rolled a joint and listened to some records. I wondered where Amos was and when he would return. And although I was happy to be given the responsibility of looking after a child, I was angry that it was his nephew and I didn't even know where to reach him if I had to. I resolved to tell him, at the first opportunity, that he was no longer welcome and must find another place to live.

I went to sleep on the couch after stripping to my briefs. But I was too restless to relax completely. I kept waking up, thinking I could hear Christopher calling me from the next room. But I checked and he was gently ensconced in dreamland.

Then, at about three o'clock in the morning, some drunkard smashed a bottle on the pavement just beneath the bedroom window. Christopher woke up and, realizing that he

133

wasn't at home, began to cry. I rushed to the bedroom and gathered him in my arms.

"It's nothing really. Some foolish person broke a bottle on the sidewalk. That's all."

"I want Mommy."

"Mommy and Daddy are in Connecticut."

He sobbed and whined, tried to flail his arms around, but I hugged him tighter and whispered, "Everything will be all right. You and I have another half a day to spend together and we can do whatever you want. Would you like to go for a walk?"

He shook his head.

"Would you like to watch television?"

"Can I?"

"Yes. There's not much on at this hour. Let's go see."

He followed me into the living room and sat on the couch. I switched on the set and reached for the *TV Guide*. An old movie with Gregory Peck and Jennifer Jones was already in progress.

"Would you like something to eat or drink?"

He nodded. I poured a glass of milk and got out a box of assorted cookies which I'd purchased just for this eventuality. He took a sip of milk, selected a chocolate creme sandwich and ate it, staring at the screen. I sat beside him and helped myself to a vanilla wafer. Before I finished chewing and swallowing he was leaning against me, asleep again. I picked him up, switched off the TV, and took him back to bed. Just as I was pulling the blanket up, he opened his eyes. "Can I sleep with you?"

I hesitated for a moment. I realized that knowledge of a mature gay man sleeping with a young boy could easily be misconstrued. But I wanted to demonstrate, to myself at least, that I could be a model parent.

"Of course, if it will make you feel better."

I got into bed and cradled him in my arms. "Sweet dreams, little man," I said and kissed the back of his neck.

I woke up at around ten o'clock Sunday morning. We were in the same position as when we'd fallen asleep. I disengaged myself and he sighed and rolled over as I rose. He entered the living room about an hour later, rubbing the sleep from his eyes with his tiny fists. His silky blond hair was askew and his briefs sagged around his knees.

"Would you like to take a shower before breakfast?"

"I always shower with Daddy on Sunday."

"Daddy isn't here."

"With you?"

We pulled off our briefs and I ran the water. I soaped him and rinsed him off. Then he did the same for me. I toweled him dry, then myself, and combed his hair.

"I was going to make some eggs and stuff, but maybe we should go somewhere for brunch. Would you like that?"

"What's brunch?"

"You'll see."

I dressed him, then myself, and we hit the almost empty sidewalk. He took my hand and we walked to a restaurant a few blocks from Sheridan Square. We were seated by a window that offered a fine view of Bleecker Street.

"Do you like Eggs Benedict?"

"What's that?"

"You'll see. If you don't like it, we'll get you something else." I realized that I was probably spoiling him, but figured one brunch wouldn't do any irreparable harm. I ordered a Bloody Mary for myself and orange juice for him.

He loved the Eggs Benedict. And hated the Bloody Mary—I let him have a small sip.

We strolled down to the river and looked at the New Jersey shore for a while and returned home. He played with his wrestler dolls until Matthew and Gloria arrived to pick him up.

Gloria took him down to the car. Matthew lingered in the doorway.

"Thank you. I hope he wasn't any trouble."

"He's a perfect gentleman and it was my pleasure."

"Where's Amos?"

"Well, he must've worked very late last night and then probably went out dancing and crashed at a friend's place."

"Would you have him call when he gets back?"

"Of course."

We shook hands and he departed.

I didn't see Amos again until two days later. I had just gotten home from the factory and was about to go to the record store when he sailed in the door.

"Hi. How're you?"

"Fine. Where've you been?"

"Around."

"I see. A few things. One, Christopher stayed here Saturday night while Matthew and Gloria went to a wedding in Connecticut. I told them you worked late and went dancing. Two, find some other place to live. You have one month, then your stuff goes out on the sidewalk and I change the locks. Understood?"

"Why?" He look perplexed.

"I don't owe you any explanations. Have I made myself clear?"

"Perfectly."

He moved in with his friend from the restaurant and I didn't see him again for several years.

*

Mike's roommate found a replacement faster than we thought he would, so Mike finally moved in. Officially. I'd gotten rid of all my accumulated junk and he — over a period of several months — moved his belongings in. Nothing changed much because he'd already been spending so much time here.

After about three months of what I thought was the perfect nonlegal marriage, we had our first fight.

The editor of a small press literary magazine was in New York for a weekend. He had just published one of my short stories and wanted to meet me. I was eager to meet him as well. We went for a drink at a bar and he complained that it was too dark and noisy to talk. So we went to an espresso cafe and ordered cappuccino and pastries.

We had a great deal to talk about — the state of literary publishing in America and the world, which books we'd read that the other ought to check out, and so on. After a couple of hours in the cafe, we had to leave because tables were needed and we wanted nothing more to eat or drink. But we had nowhere to go. I suggested that we go to my apartment and finish our discussion.

Mike was watching television when we arrived and greeted us icily. The editor and I went into the bedroom and we talked for another two hours. When we emerged, Mike was still angry and was — I thought — rather rude to our departing guest. He didn't say another word to me that night but went straight to bed. The next morning I confronted him.

"You were nasty to me and my guest last night."

"You were rude to bring him here without calling first."

So that was it. I thought he was jealous because he suspected we'd done something sexual. "I'm sorry. I didn't think of that. We had no place else to go. He doesn't like bars and we still had lots to talk about. I'm sorry, but I didn't think twice about just coming home."

"Look, you're not living alone anymore. You have to consider me too. All you had to do was call and let me know you were coming and everything would have been fine."

"I'm sorry. I wasn't thinking."

We kissed like gouramis and hugged like magnets. "C'mere, sweet thing," he said. And we made love. A gesture of forgiveness. An expression of feelings that can not manifest themselves in any other way. Sex, all by itself, can be glorious. With someone you love, it's sublime. And making up after a spat is arguably the best that one can expect from the flesh. Not that people should fight to improve their sex lives. It's just the best way I know to let someone know you still care.

*

Jennifer was in her eighth month and we had completed the Lamaze training. She had overthrown all of her bad habits — as far as smoking, drinking, and snorting were involved — and hadn't seen Max in quite some time. We decided to pay a visit. Jennifer called and asked if we could attend an Etiquette class.

Max was dressed in a sari with a repeating floral pattern. Frankincense wafted from a ceramic burner shaped like a Buddha and sitar music permeated the room. Jennifer and I sat on the couch. She folded her hands over her large tummy. Max pirouetted and placed his right hand on his hip.

"Well? How do I look?"

"Who're you supposed to be?" I asked.

"Indira Gandhi, who else?" he said flippantly.

Jennifer laughed. "What's the occasion?"

"The Power Drag Ball."

"Power Drag Ball, what's that?" she giggled.

"All the guests must masquerade as a woman of power. I was thinking of doing Margaret Thatcher but *everyone* will probably do her. Then I thought of Eva Peron, but again, there'll probably be a hundred queens in rented *Evita* costumes."

"You could do Lady MacBeth," I suggested.

"Or Nancy Reagan," said Jennifer with a smirk.

"I said women of power. Not beasts with wimpy husbands." He sat across from us and lit a joint. Jennifer refused it but I took a long drag.

"We miss you around here, honey," said Max.

"I'm not doing drugs anymore," she said, patting her belly.

"You can still drop by for a visit."

"I will."

"Good." He turned to me. "I bought myself a guitar and a lesson book. It ain't as easy as it looks."

"The hardest part is at the beginning because your hands aren't used to it. It gets easier. Just give it time."

He took a deep hit and blew out streaming billows of gray smoke. "I'm going to go to Nashville and cut a demo," he said.

"Really?"

"Uh, huh."

He went to the stereo and removed the sitar cassette. He inserted another and poised himself as though before a microphone. The song was "Blue Moon Of Kentucky" by Patsy Cline. And rather than lip sync, he sang along at full volume. He had mastered the intricacies of country vocal stylization. The swoops, sighs, glottal stops, and phrasing. At times he sounded like Patsy — he had her growl down pat — and some of the notes had a teary catch like Tammy Wynette. Jennifer looked at me in amazement.

"He sounds like a real southern broad," she exclaimed.

We applauded his performance and he curtsied.

"Thank y'all," he stretched out the syllables, "this here next number was a big hit for the lovely Miss Loretta Lynn. It's gone from the charts but still in your hearts."

He launched into "You Ain't Woman Enough (To Take My Man)." He may have been dressed like Indira Gandhi, but he sounded just like Loretta. Jennifer and I were speechless. It was one of the Quintessential Maxian Moments. One that I rely on when trying to describe Max to a friend who hasn't met him.

*

After Lorenzo died, Donald melted into a severe depression that lasted several months. He rarely called, and if I called him, he sounded forlorn.

"I'm not very good company right now," he said. "At first I was miserable because I'd lost the best man I'd ever

139

had. Now I'm worried about myself. My tests have all been negative, but no one is sure how long the incubation period is so I could wake up one morning in two years and find out I've got it. Even if I never have sex again."

"First of all, that's true of all of us. Anyone can develop AIDS at this stage. That's no reason to stop living."

"Life without sex is not *worth* living," he growled.

"There are ways of having sex without endangering yourself or others."

"How would you know? You and Mike are having a very satisfying sex life."

"That's true. But we could also be killing each other. If I hadn't met Mike and was still single, I'd be using condoms and refraining from certain, uh, activities."

"That's easy for you to say."

"No, it's not. Nothing's permanent. Mike and I could break up tomorrow and then I'd be in the same position as you." He was silent. I tried to change the subject. "Are you getting any painting done?"

"I'm too upset to concentrate."

"Would you like to get together? Dinner or a movie?"

"I want to see this new play about AIDS. *The Normal Heart.* I think that's what it's called. Maybe it'll make me feel better."

"It might make you feel worse."

"I'll risk it."

"Why don't I get tickets for the three of us? I know Mike wants to see it too. It might be a good way for you to meet him."

"Sounds good."

"I'll get tickets and give you a call."

"Okay."

"Talk to you soon," I said and hung up the phone.

*

Shortly after I became music editor of the *Clarion*, the publisher created a new position — arts editor. This welcome change allowed the editor, Lee, to concentrate on political coverage — especially AIDS-related news — and made for a good balance between art, music, dance, film, theater, and literature. Prior to this, the arts coverage was scattershot.

My new boss was Lucy. She'd started out writing theater reviews. I'd never met her before — though I'd read her stuff — and when she called to announce that she was to be my immediate superior, I was a bit frightened at first. What if she didn't like my work? What if she had a friend who wanted to be music editor? I worried about the answers to those questions until I went to meet her at the *Clarion* office.

She was short and slender, with long, brown hair and big, beautiful eyes. She rose to shake my hand, then sat behind her desk, which supported a nameplate that said "Lucy Jenkins — Editrix."

"A gift from my lover," she explained, "to start off on the right foot, or the left foot, as the case may be." She quickly went on to inform me that her lover, Deborah, was a professional triathlete, traveled a lot, and that they'd been together for six years.

"What I want to do," she said, "is bring some organization to our arts coverage. Up until now, it's been kind of a hit-or-miss thing and I want to stabilize it so that we have two pages of reviews on a variety of music events every issue. I'm telling the same thing to all the other arts editors. It's your job to choose who will review what, and to keep it varied so that all kinds of music events are covered. It's my job to coordinate the entire arts section and make sure that timely reviews don't get postponed because of too many political articles."

Well, I said to myself, Lee may not be thrilled about this new arrangement, but I was overjoyed. I breathed deeply, relieved that I hadn't been summarily dismissed. Glad that the *Clarion*'s arts coverage might have a chance at some respectability.

Thanks to Lucy, my job became easier. Previously, if the editor or publisher decided that a fast-breaking story about say, congressional sex scandals, was more important than the review of the new production of Wagner's *Ring*, the music review would get bumped. Postponed to a later issue. I'd, of course, get irate phone calls from the critic and the opera company.

"Gee, I'm sorry," I'd explain, "but the editor just didn't have the space. There was nothing I could do. Believe me."

Then they'd yell and scream for a while and I'd assure them that the review would appear the following week.

When Lucy took over, the irate phone calls ceased and I found I had a lot less hassles to deal with.

*

We're in the thick of winter right now. The apartment is drafty and no amount of caulking seems to help. We considered putting plastic sheeting over the windows but that would destroy our view. When we're in bed, our combined body heat keeps us warm. But when we're not, we have to wear several layers of clothing to stay comfortable. Mike and I are spending a lot of time in bed these days.

Down on the street, the people move about very quickly. Some days it's so cold people rush from door to door, trying to avoid being in the cold any longer than is absolutely necessary. And, as though the temperature weren't bad enough, the humidity and wind only add to a climate that is almost unbearable.

No one looks sexy these days. Everyone is bundled into leg warmers, parkas, gloves, hats, ski masks, mufflers, and ear muffs which bring a shapeless androgyny to even the most perfect bodies.

I wonder why New York couldn't be where Miami is, or Los Angeles. If the seasonal changes weren't so drastic, New York could be a delight the year around. But the winters are too cold, the summers are too hot, and what lies between is too brief.

If I had a lot of money I'd winter down south and summer in New England. But that's just a dream. I'd have to write a book called *Cats, Dieting, and the Road to Wealth*, or a romance-spy novel that takes place on seven continents, to earn the money to make the dream come true. But I don't want to do that. I don't think I could. Besides, there are plenty of writers covering that material. I want to write the stories that no one else is writing. I may have fewer readers than a best-selling author, but at least I'll be filling a void. Providing something that you can't get just anywhere. And that's better than a dream of luxury. Any day. I think. Or hope.

—— Chapter Thirteen ——

Jennifer phoned me — I was at the box office — at approximately three o'clock on a Wednesday afternoon. "It's started."

"What started?"

"The contractions. I can feel the pitter patter of little feet all over my insides. I'm packed and ready to go to the hospital."

"Should I come over or meet you there?"

"I'm on my way."

I hung up the phone. "It's special delivery time," I said to my co-treasurers. I grabbed my jacket and sailed out the door.

I entered the hospital with the usual disgust. As if the antiseptic white walls and overpowering smell of detergent weren't enough, seeing bleeding, battered bodies going by on gurneys made my stomach queasy. But I got to the delivery room with my lunch intact.

Jennifer was already flat on her back, in a starched hospital gown, with her legs up in stirrups. A layer of beaded sweat covered her forehead. Her hair was pulled back from her face.

I was ushered into a changing room by Dr. Gilbert and donned the gown, gloves, and mask. When I emerged the doctor said, "The contractions are coming closer now. This could be over before we know it."

I moved to Jennifer's side and grasped her hand. She gripped me so tightly my fingers were numb a few moments later. Her breaths were deep and hard and her entire face was streaked with perspiration. We synchronized our breathing and established the rhythmic pattern we'd practiced for months. Dr. Gilbert examined her uterus and mumbled, "Fine, fine, everything is going well."

My mind began to spin and I tried to focus on the breathing. Every time I looked at Jennifer I wanted to turn away. The look on her face — eyes wide, mouth gasping, forehead crinkled — was it ecstacy or despair? I couldn't decide if she was feeling pleasure or pain. Whether I should smile or try to look sympathetic. I guess my face was just blank. Then I began to sweat. I could feel my heart, like a wrecking ball in double time.

"It's gonna be all right," Jennifer gasped.

"That's what I'm supposed to tell you," I said and Dr. Gilbert laughed.

Jennifer howled. I clutched her hand tighter.

"It's all right," muttered the doctor.

Jennifer moaned and her body began to shake.

"It's coming, it's coming," she screamed and the look on her face reflected naked terror.

"Push!" the doctor commanded, "push!" and Jennifer groaned as she worked her muscles. I was soaked at this point. Jennifer was too. The doctor said, "Head's out, you're doing fine. Push!"

Jennifer writhed and wailed. I felt suffocated, as though the air was being sucked from the room.

"Push!" the doctor said again. "Good! Push!"

The next thing I knew, Jennifer screamed and broke into a wide smile. Her eyes filled with tears and overflowed.

The doctor held Magda up and I looked at the tiny body

with blue veins and sticky limbs. I gasped and said, "I think I'm going to faint," as my mind whirled into darkness.

"That's not unusual," I heard the doctor say.

The floor came rushing up to my face and the next thing I remember was waking up in the waiting room. Dr. Gilbert was holding my hand and held a wet cloth to my forehead.

"How's Jennifer?" I asked groggily.

"She's fine."

"And the baby?"

"She's fine too. It's you we were worried about. You lie still. Drink some of this."

She brought a glass of cold water to my lips.

"When can I see her?"

"She's sleeping now. When you feel up to it you ought to go home and get some rest. You can come and see her tomorrow."

*

About two week after Amos moved out I got a call from Gloria.

"How are you?" she asked cautiously.

"I'm fine," I said, "and you?"

"Fine."

"And Matthew and Christopher?"

"We're all fine."

"Good."

There was a long, uncomfortable pause that lasted for what seemed like forever.

"The reason I called is, well, I was wondering if you wanted to tell me what happened with Amos. We know he moved out but he wouldn't say why."

My stomach tightened. This was what I had been dreading. Part of me wanted to tell her what a monster her brother-in-law could be. The other part of me didn't want to talk about it. Just try to forget.

"I don't know what to say. I don't want to go into the

gory details. It just didn't work out. We didn't have as much in common as we thought."

"I see."

No you don't see, I wanted to say, you only see his good side.

"I hope you'll stay in touch with us," she said.

"Gloria, I'm really glad that I got to know you and Matthew and I had a great time with Christopher when he stayed over—"

"He talks about you all the time. Every Sunday he compares my breakfasts with the brunch you treated him to."

"The pleasure was all mine."

"He also said that Amos never came home in all the time he was there."

I wanted the conversation to end. "Give my best to Matthew and Christopher and take good care of yourself, okay?"

"Okay."

"Bye now."

"Bye."

With Amos gone I was able to think about other things. I spent some time gazing out the window, trying to assess my position and determine where I wanted to go. I was beginning to feel more secure about my potential as a writer and was becoming more disillusioned with the music business. I hated the factory but needed the money, liked the record store but it wasn't enough to live on. I was also free to cruise and make new acquaintances.

I decided that I had two major priorities. The first was to start actively seeking some new kind of job and the second was to ease myself back into circulation. Every morning I'd pick up the newspaper, skip the news items, and turn directly to the classified ads. Every evening I went to a different bar or disco. The job market looked bleak, but there were attractive men everywhere.

One night I entered a disco that I'd never been to before. I ordered a cocktail and sipped it at the bar. I noticed a guy

—very handsome with chiseled features, blond hair, and a perfect tan—looking at me, so I smiled. He smiled back and walked through the crowd that separated us. He held out his hand.

"Hi. My name's Carl."

I introduced myself and asked if he came there often because I didn't know what else to say.

"Too often," he said, grinning. Beautiful teeth.

"What do you do?" I asked, fearing that a silence was about to come between us.

"I'm in market research. The company I work for transferred me here about six months ago. I didn't like it at first, but I'm getting used to it."

"Where are you from?"

"Oregon. You from around here?"

"Yes."

"What do you do?"

"I work at a factory during the day, a record store at night, and on the weekends I split my time between music and writing."

"What kind of music?"

"I'm a singer/songwriter."

"And what do you write?"

"Music reviews and short stories."

We danced for a while. It was nice. The dance floor was packed with hot, sweaty bodies. Naked torsos flexed, tightly-jeaned buns bounced up and down, and the scent of poppers filled the air. The music was loud and all-consuming. Bass lines vibrated through the soles of our running shoes, a black female voice soared into the stratosphere.

As the time went by we became more suggestive with our body language until, eventually, we were hugging and kissing, grinding our hips together in the center of the dance floor. I pulled back from a deep kiss and asked if he wanted to go to my apartment.

We had a memorable night of get-down, uninhibited, sweaty, pre-AIDS sex and started to see each other about two times a week. This went on for several months, until he called one day and asked if I was free the following Thursday.

"Well, that's not so good," I said. "I've been invited over to my aunt and uncle's for Passover."

"Passover?"

"Yes, they always invite me over to dinner for Passover and Rosh Hashanna."

"You're Jewish?" he asked, astonished.

"Yes."

"I didn't know that. You certainly don't look it."

I actually think he meant that as some kind of compliment, but my built-in bullshit detector registered a serious tremor. "Thursday's no good, but Wednesday's fine. I get out of work at ten."

"Gee, I don't know, Wednesday doesn't look so good, I'll give you a call. Bye."

Needless to say, that was the last of Carl.

Undaunted, I kept going out. One night, hanging out at the Corral, I met Billy. Short and muscular, with a clone mustache and a cleft chin. When he innocently said, "Tell me about yourself," I seized the opportunity.

"Well," I said nervously, "I'm Jewish," and paused to see if he would bolt. He remained where he stood.

"So am I," he said, "I hope you won't hold it against me."

We laughed. Bought drinks and chatted about theater. He was the business manager at an off-Broadway theater and when he invited me to go to his apartment, I accepted.

*

Although I was making regular appearances in the music section of the *Clarion*, I wasn't getting paid very much. So when the editor of a rival magazine phoned and asked if I'd be interested in writing a book review column — for a monthly fee that was more than I could earn at the *Clarion* in a year — I said yes without hesitation. After I'd hung up the phone, I suddenly thought of a lot of questions. Such as, how did he even know I'd be capable of writing a book review column? After all, until then I'd only written about music. And how did he get my phone number? I didn't suppose he called the *Clarion* office and told them he wanted to try to lure away the music editor.

I pushed these questions aside and started contacting publishers so I could get review copies of new books. When I introduced myself to the publicity agents and told them I was writing for *Beefcake* magazine, some of them snickered and said, "Oh really, what's that?" When I replied, "A magazine for upwardly mobile gay men with large discretionary incomes," the snickers stopped. And the books began to arrive in the mail.

I decided to quit the *Clarion*, but before that happened I finally succeeded in accomplishing something concrete in the area of gay cultural politics. I convinced the Metropolitan Opera Company to provide opening night press comps to the *Clarion*'s opera critics.

Initially, my opera critics would only write about the operas they were going to attend anyway, because the Met refused to put us on their press list. I wrote several letters which received cool responses, informing me that the *Clarion* wasn't a significant enough paper to merit press consideration. I kept writing letters until they finally agreed to occasionally service us on a third or fourth night.

But that wasn't good enough for me. So I wrote a rather angry letter in which I queried: "Have you ever bothered to observe which people constitute the majority of your audience? Seventy-five percent of the opera fans in this city are gay males. All you have to do is stroll through the lobby during intermission to verify this. The *Clarion* is New York's gay paper. Your audience is primarily gay. That you would deny us opening night press comps is as stupid as it is unfair."

It worked.

Lee and Lucy were thrilled about my victory with the Met.

And not so thrilled that I was quitting the *Clarion* and working for *Beefcake*.

I changed gears overnight. Or so it seemed. The music critic became a book reviewer. And the books began to pile up. One of my chief problems these days is figuring where to put them. Right now, they're stacked everywhere. I'll have to start weeding out my record collection. There's a lot of records that I never listen to anymore. And an entire stack that I never got around to listening to even once. I used to imagine that someday I'd go back and spend some time with the unexplored vinyl. But right now I have to create space for all the new books. I guess a lot of the records will have to go.

*

Directly across the street, just beyond the park, is a new gay disco which used to be a nightclub offering Middle Eastern entertainment. Around the time the park was renovated, the nightclub was sold to a gay entrepreneur who owns a chain of discos and restaurants. The building was refurbished and converted into a gay emporium with a piano bar at street level and a disco downstairs. The funny thing was that prior to the facelift, busloads of middle-aged and elderly suburbanites — mostly from the old country — would disembark and spend Sunday afternoons eating Middle Eastern food, listening to Mediterranean lounge singers. For several months after the metamorphosis, the busloads of people — not yet aware that the old club was defunct — would mill about on the sidewalk, shocked to find that their old gathering place had been converted into a high-tech disco. I'd smoke a joint and watch the people — old ladies wringing their hands and stooped men shaking their heads — wondering how such a thing could happen. I felt sorry for them.

I thought of the times when I made plans to meet a friend at a favorite restaurant and we'd discover, upon arriving, that it was gone and a boutique or greengrocer had taken its place. It was no big deal for us, though. We'd simply eat someplace else. But a busload of people from the suburbs, expecting an afternoon in a familiar setting that had disappeared, had no other choices. They simply got back on the bus and returned home. I wondered why they didn't phone ahead to confirm whether there would be enough room. Perhaps another busload of people from a different suburb had rented the entire place for the afternoon?

But times change, things progress, and all of us are victims at one time or another. I wonder what disappointments I'll have to face as I grow older. Not too many, I hope. Still, it's inevitable.

*

Mike had been living with me for about two months when he announced that he'd been hired to design sets for the new production of *Lucia Di Lammermoor* at the City Opera. Until then, he'd mainly designed off-Broadway productions — with an occasional TV or film assignment. But this was his big break.

He worked very hard on this project. Long hours of intense, back-breaking, mind-numbing work. For the three days prior to opening, he was forced to stay at the theater day and night, working around the clock.

We rented tuxedos for the opening night gala and took a taxi to Lincoln Center. The lobby was packed with people in formal attire, but there were gay guys in full leather regalia as well. Gowns, jewels, and furs mingled alongside chaps, studs, and rear-pocket hankies. A typical opening night at the opera.

Mike fetched us champagne from the bar. When the lights flickered, we took our seats and waited for the curtain to rise.

The orchestra played the overture and Mike held my hand as the performers assembled on stage. The first set depicted the craggy ruins of the Ravenswood Estate, and Mike's design looked eerie and forbidding.

The big voices filled the auditorium, telling the story of thwarted lust and passion. I was swept away by the grandeur of it all. I cried when the diva — whom I'd never heard of before — sang the famous mad scene aria, wringing pathos from every note. Her gestures were subtle and she acted with far more finesse than most of the divas I'd seen previously.

As the final notes faded away, Mike and I leapt to our feet and applauded enthusiastically. The soprano took three curtain calls and when the ovations were over, Mike led us backstage. He tried to introduce me to several people but he was overwhelmed by well-wishers who lavished praise on his set designs. I felt so proud.

Afterwards, we taxied back downtown and went to the Corral. The bartender almost dropped a bottle of gin when we strutted in wearing tuxes. We kept laughing at the faces of the newcomers whose surprise could not be concealed when they noticed the tuxedos tucked in among the denim, muscle shirts, and jingle-jangle key rings.

*

If Aliens are anything like Earthlings, there must be three kinds: the exceptional, the average, and the pathetic. I try to imagine one of each kind as a customer at the box office. It helps pass the time when things are slow.

The exceptional one would politely inquire as to what's available, and would quickly realize, from my descriptions, that many of the shows that we handle are not worth the time one would spend to sit through them. It would thank me for my time and go look for tickets to a concert or a baseball game.

An Average Alien, curious about theatrical culture on Earth, would purchase a ticket to a drama or comedy that I would recommend and probably enjoy, if not the play, the audience during intermission. Though realizing it had not witnessed anything spectacular, it would be grateful for the uniqueness of the experience.

The pathetic Alien, a stowaway perhaps or a wealthy heir doomed to idiocy from too much inbreeding, would stand at the window, translator in hand (or claw, paw, tentacle, or whatever) and ask what it is that I'm selling.

"Theater tickets, off-Broadway."

"What's a theater ticket?"

"It's a piece of paper that allows you entry to see a fictionalized recreation of life on Earth."

It thinks for a minute, a spittle of drool creeping down its chin.

"You mean, like a religious rite?"

"Sort of. A writer creates a script that actors memorize and perform with sets, lights, and costumes. Some make you laugh, some make you cry, some can do both."

"I want to laugh."

I sell it a ticket for that evening.

The next day the Alien is back at the box office.

"I didn't laugh," it complains.

Neither did the critics, I want to say, but then it will ask what a critic is and I don't have the time or patience for that.

"Well, I'm sorry, but I guess these plays are created for Earthlings and Aliens just can't appreciate them."

"I want my money back."

If this were an Earthling I'd point to the 'No Refunds' sign and tell him or her that there's nothing I can do. But I refund the Alien's money — and absorb the cost of the ticket myself — to foster convivial intergalactic relations. Then I suggest that it go see an evening of championship wrestling.

—— Chapter Fourteen ——

Mike and I have been socializing a lot lately with Donald and his new lover, Benjamin. Both of them had lovers who died of AIDS-related illnesses. And both volunteered to help the Gay Men's Health Crisis — a support group formed to help victims, and their lovers and families, cope with the many problems this disease can cause. Benjamin recently moved into Donald's apartment on Sullivan Street. They seem to be doing fine.

Benjamin is twenty-eight-years-old and works for a real estate agency. He has mahogany skin, high cheek bones, and full, sensual lips. His body is agile and angular, his wit sharp.

The four of us see lots of science fiction films together, usually in conjunction with a protracted meal at a nice restaurant. Benjamin is an expert in fantasy/science fiction/horror books, and films. He leads us to the winners and instinctively knows what to avoid. I'm looking forward to getting to know him better.

*

I had several dates with Billy — the second guy I met after Amos moved out — and we always had a good time together. He had a terrific sense of humor and never failed to make me laugh whenever he wanted to. I'd known him about a month when we had a conversation one night after losing ourselves in wild sex. After the waves of sensation subsided, reality flowed back into my conscious thoughts.

"I've got to get out of the factory. I don't think I can stand it another day."

Billy looked at me with his puppy-like eyes as though I'd just read his mind. "Funny you should mention it," he said, "but I have a friend who runs an off-Broadway box office and he's looking for a new treasurer. Apparently most of the people who apply are actors and they quit as soon as they get a part. He wants someone who'll be around for a while." He looked at me, wondering if he should continue.

"Go on."

"He called today and said he's desperate for a non-actor who is dependable, organized, and polite. I immediately thought of you."

"Does this person have to have prior experience?"

"No."

"Do you really think I can handle it?"

"Yes."

"I don't know anything about box office work."

"You'd be handling large sums of money and obnoxious people."

"The people I can deal with. But I was the worst math student imaginable."

"This is the eighties. They use calculators."

"What do you think?" I asked.

"I think you should apply."

Billy set up an appointment for me and the next thing I knew, I was a box office treasurer. It took a few days for me to feel secure about what I was doing, but within a week I was able to handle all the aspects of the operation. The first lesson I learned was not to panic. Many situations arise which seem insurmountable and your first reaction is to lose control. But these tangles always work themselves out if you remain cool enough not to make them any worse.

Things didn't quite work out so well with Billy, though. He began spending more time at his office. Sometimes putting in an eighteen-hour day. And he was so tired most of the time, all he wanted to do was sleep. I cajoled him, and finally begged him to slow down but he insisted that if he was going to get anywhere, he'd have to demonstrate his dedication and stamina.

I'd sit around waiting for him to leave work night after night. He'd rarely show up and when he did he was exhausted. He'd always apologize profusely but I began to get lonely. He said it was okay for me to date other guys, but that's not what I wanted. I was hoping that Billy might be what Amos was not. That we'd live together for a long time in peaceful happiness. But Billy was too career-minded to settle down.

Eventually we drifted apart. I thought that once my relationship with him was over, that I'd be fired from the box office. But the boss was pleased with my work, I finally found out, which allayed my fears that I was hired simply because Billy requested it.

We're still friends but rarely see each other. I get a Christmas card every year, though.

*

Spring finally arrived and Mike and I uncaulked the windows and packed away our winter-wear. It feels good to be in light, comfortable clothing again. Given the choice between a brand new sweater and an old, faded T-shirt, I'll take the T-shirt every time.

Sheridan Square is blooming. Slow moving tourists and fast moving natives are crowding the sidewalks again. Loud ghetto blasters offer snatches of the latest rap tunes and nightfall usually brings a chorus of winos who yell at each other and beg spare change from the passersby. The police try to discourage them but they are a hardy and persistent bunch.

157

The trees in the park are beginning to show green buds. Some of the adjacent flowers have already opened up. As the sun lends warmth and nourishment to the new leaves, this apartment will once more offer the illusion of a treehouse paradise where happy children play, oblivious to all worldly cares. A flick of the radio switch still brings a litany of international tragedies, but I manage to dispel these images and return to my typewriter.

*

When Max returned from Nashville, he phoned and invited me to the Charm School for afternoon tea. He greeted me at the door wearing white overalls and a purple T-shirt that said "Tough Shit." The only noticeable aroma was that of marijuana.

I sat on the couch. He rolled a joint. The stereo was silent.

"That's some weird town," he said, licking the flap and twisting the ends. "The gay bars have wonderful drag shows — lots of cute southern boys too. But the music industry people are really fucked up."

"How so?"

"They're living in the past. As though the Civil War never happened." He passed me the joint.

"What do you mean?"

"You heard my demo. What did you think?"

"I think it's great. As good as any modern country I've heard."

"They are definitely not ready for a black female country star. Generic or otherwise."

"What are you going to do?"

"Save up some money, make another demo — you and I are going to write a killer song together — and try again."

I tried to picture Max in cowgirl drag pitching his tape to the Entrepreneurs of Country Music. I wondered if they could tell that he's a transvestite? Did they reject him because of his tape or because of his outfit? Or was it the skin tone?

I'll bet most of them couldn't even tell he was a man in a dress.

"Charley Pride and Ray Charles are the only black folks that regularly get on country radio," he continued, "why are black women still excluded?"

"I don't know. It could be sexism or racism or both." He sighed. "Both probably."

I thought about this as I walked home that evening. I wasn't worried about Max — he's a fighter who always gets back to his feet. But I worry about institutions that refuse to grow and adapt to the changes taking place all around. The future of American pop music is, I'm afraid, depressing. Radio is still largely segregated. Record companies are afraid to take chances on unusual acts. Consumers are content to swallow whatever junk — no matter how half-baked or overcooked — the promoters are serving. And the artists have to struggle so hard just to get heard, when and if they finally break through, all they can think about is maintaining solvency. Creativity never has a chance to enter their minds. Who has time to think about art when sales, promotion, touring, chart positions, contract negotiations, and video considerations are all that really matter? The system that worships mediocrity and rejects originality may never change. At least as long as it's encouraged by the public. And a truly significant change would require major restructuring from the bottom up. A return to the beginning. Not likely at this stage.

*

One night while Mike was out of town — supervising the construction of his set designs for a production of *Amadeus* in Salt Lake City — I went out for a drink and ran into Amos.

His hair was longer, his eyes looked tired, and he had a bruise on his lip. He came over to me and cautiously said hello.

"Hello," I said.

"How are you?"

"Fine," I said. "You?"

"Okay. I'm still at Cafe In The Park. Getting tired of it, though."

"How are Matthew and Gloria and Christopher?"

"They're great. They moved away. Living in Denver now. Chris is so tall. You wouldn't recognize him."

I didn't know what to say.

"I'm thinking of moving back to New Orleans." He paused for several moments. "You're probably wondering about this cut on my lip."

I didn't say anything. Didn't want him to know I was curious. He might think I still cared.

"The guy I've been living with —"

"Sandy, right?"

"No, I'm living with someone else now. He beats me up sometimes. I just want you to know that I gave you a lot more reason to hit me and you never did. I appreciate that. And I'm sorry for all the dumb things I did to you."

He waited for me to accept his apology. But I couldn't. I knew that the proper thing to do would be to forgive. But something in me prevented my doing so. "Take care, Amos," was the best I could manage. I turned away and went to another bar.

I stood there sipping a cocktail and relived my time with Amos. The thing I could never figure out was whether he ever truly loved me and fell out of love upon arriving in New York. Or if he never loved me and simply used me to get here. It's a question that I still think about any time Amos comes to mind. Which happens now and then. If someone mentions New Orleans, Mardi Gras, jambalaya, or Dixieland jazz. I ask myself if he ever loved me. I guess I'll never really know. I try not to let it bother me.

*

The American public has finally become aware of the fact that AIDS is as potentially dangerous to them as it is to gay men. At last, progress is being made at the national level. People who were completely ignorant of the facts are learning the truth. And I believe straight people's desire to protect themselves will generate enough money so that all of us will benefit.

When the disease was perceived as being limited to certain groups — with gay men being singled out as culprits instead of victims — everything looked hopeless. But there appears to be a new attitude that suggests that we're all in this together. That should make everything in this country more pleasant for everyone.

In fact, the entire planet is becoming aware of this disease and simultaneously, with the plight of gay people. It's an exorbitant price to pay, but it's possible that this illness will ultimately do more for gay liberation than all of the marching, lobbying, and legislation on which gay leaders have spent most of their time.

*

I'm still working at Ticket Pandemonium, but I'm hoping that I'll get out fairly soon. I finally heard from the publisher about my manuscript of short stories. He likes them and wants to publish them, but I know this will take time. And once a date is set, the likelihood is such that it will not appear on schedule. I have learned that this is the way most things on Earth operate. You do your best then you must wait. And wait.

But getting published will not only provide some income, it is also possible that certain doors may open. Like teaching literature and creative writing. Giving readings and lectures.

And who knows? Some producer or agent may want to turn one of my stories into a play or movie. That would be welcome news.

I think the time will come that I will be able to write full time. Until then, I will continue to derive pleasure from seeing my stories in literary magazines. There's no money involved, but it's good to know that someone considers my stuff worthy of the paper, ink, and printing costs that it takes to publish a periodical. And presumably, someone out there is reading my work. I hope that he, she, it, or they will enjoy it. The only thing a writer can ask is that someone read what he has bothered to write. The whole idea is to communicate. If a story is not published, then it cannot be read. Getting a story published offers the writer a glimmer of hope.

*

Mike and I were sipping coffee, watching wrestling on TV. Saturday morning. Lovely day. Randy "Macho Man" Savage was beating the shit out of Paul Roma. Or so we were supposed to believe. But it didn't matter. The pleasure lies in watching those built-up, tanned bodies and listening to the outrageous commentary.

The telephone rang and Mike jumped up to answer it.

"Hello?" Pause. "Hi, Jennifer." Pause. "We're fine, how're you?" Pause. "That's good, and Magda and Russell?" Pause. "Hold on."

He handed me the receiver. "What's up?"

"Well," she began, "it's not working out at all. I quit the soap last night because I got a wonderful offer to be a part of a new repertory company. I'll make enough to pay the bills — we're not talking big bucks here — and I'll have more time for Magda. The pace is killing me and I don't want to become a stranger to my daughter."

For two weeks she'd been up every morning at four o'clock, out by six, and didn't get home until early evening. Russell would wake up at six and stay with Magda until Jennifer's mother arrived at noon. She would stay until Jennifer or Russell got back home. By then Magda was asleep.

"You may be making less money, but I consider the move from TV to theater to be a step up rather than down."

"You're probably right."

That was the beginning of a new phase in all our lives.

Rehearsals for productions at the Phoenix Theater never start until around noon. This gives Jennifer and Magda —almost four years old—the mornings to spend together. When a play begins performances, the curtain is at eight, giving mother and daughter entire days to themselves.

Russell had, by this time, quit The Revulsionz and become a singer of commercial jingles. If he has a recording session in the afternoon and Jennifer has to rehearse also, one of them drops Magda off at our apartment. If I'm at the box office that day, Mike spends the afternoon with her. He usually takes her to a museum, for walks in the park, or they watch videos together. If I'm off that day, Magda stays here with me. I'll read to her for a while, then we'll play games. Eventually she's looking at picture books while I'm typing.

I expect this routine to continue until Magda starts school. Right now, it's ideal. Jennifer and Russell have two reliable baby sitters. Mike and I have a surrogate daughter. And Magda gets to hang out with four different adults. Everyone is happy with this arrangement.

*

I hope the Aliens will arrive soon. I'm convinced that they'll probably get to Earth before we can get to their planet. And who knows what they'll have to offer us, aside from the spectacle and the promise of something new and exciting. They may have knowledge and wisdom to impart. Perhaps even a cure for AIDS.

I hope they won't flee out of fear that the bad habits of Earthlings are contagious. Or lose control, laughing themselves silly when confronted with the enormity of human folly.

But when and if they do arrive, I wish I could be the one to deliver an address of welcome.

"Greetings," I would say, "and welcome." I check the indicator light of my pocket translator to make sure it's working properly. "This is the planet Earth, third from the center of our solar system. I am an Earthling and I am as typical

163

of my race as I am peculiar. You will find good and bad here. But part of the fun is sorting it all out.

"Are you tired? If so, rest first, we'll talk later.

"Are you hungry? I'm not sure what you consider edible, but I know a fabulous place where they make the best beef stroganoff anywhere. Of course, if you're vegetarian there are other places we can go. Shall I call for reservations?"

—— Chapter Fifteen ——

I was sitting on a bench in Sheridan Square Park. Something I'd never done before, even though it was directly across the street from me for over five years. Probably because of a lack of time coupled with an aversion for the park's sleazy denizens. The trees provided shade from the glaring sun and a cool breeze from the Hudson River provided some relief. Max had called and said we should meet in the park. He was leaving for Nashville on the following day. "I'm gonna make it in that town someday. I'm gonna be a black country star." The plan was to smoke a joint together and say goodbye. But he arrived late and I had the opportunity to observe the park — and my building — from a different point of view.

Cars rushing by, the sidewalks jammed with bodies, the park is like the inside of a whirlpool. All the detritus swirls around the vortex, inexorably drawn to the center. A couple of drunks were sitting on a bench opposite me, passing around a bottle of something. A middle-aged woman, shabbily dressed, was reading a yellowed newspaper and some street kid had passed out and was sleeping it off — whatever *it* was — stretched out on the brick parquet. At the entrance-way, four girls in motorcycle jackets, rhinestone-studded sunglasses, and pedal pushers sang a doo wop song from the early sixties. Adjacent to them, a squad of beggars were bumming loose change from pedestrians and the drivers of cars that had to stop for the red light.

I glanced at the doorway to my building as my downstairs neighbor emerged. A Turkish man who plays tenor saxophone, he moved in shortly after I did, replacing the elderly woman named Rose who had died several days after my arrival. On the fifth floor is a Cuban man who writes film critiques for the *Village Voice*. Across the hall from us is a young man whom I think is a hustler — the traffic to and from his apartment rivals the assortment of hot gay men that wanders through the West Village every day. But this is merely conjecture. Perhaps he's a rich heir, simply promiscuous, and money never changes hands. On the floor below, opposite the sax player, is a man — about forty, I'd say — who I only see on weekends and is frequently visited by a woman and three girls who I assume are the wife and daughters from whom he is separated. On the first floor lives a dancer whom I rarely see — she travels a lot with a modern dance company — and whomever lives across the hall from her, I couldn't say as I've never seen this person. The apartment could be empty for all I know; I've never seen anyone coming or going and I've never heard a sound from within. Mike calls it The Tomb Of The Beatnik Poet.

Max arrived and sat beside me. Dressed in tight jeans and an orange tanktop, his sinewy body looked invitingly masculine deprived of feminine apparel. He crossed his long legs and produced a joint. Just then, a mangy bag lady — a transvestite actually — ambled by. Wearing a floral print granny dress.

"That's mine," said Max in a hushed voice. "I threw that out a few weeks ago. I'd recognize it anywhere. I bet she found it going through my trash."

We smoked the joint as the angle of sunlight slanting through the trees shifted slowly.

"I'm flying to Nashville tomorrow and I just wanted to say goodbye," he kissed my cheek, "and say thanks for tutoring me."

"I'll miss you."

"I'll be back. But I gotta do what I gotta do."

I nodded and wished him good luck.

"I'll send you copies of all my demo tapes. And when I cut my first album, you'll get the first one that's pressed."

"Maybe we'll write a country song together sometime, like we talked about."

"Sugar, I just know we will."

A new wave lady passed by with a Mohawk haircut dyed metallic blue. Max snorted and whispered to me, "Who styles *her* hair? Must be someone from Mars."

We laughed and walked to the pier, all the while commenting on the incredible sidewalk parade.

*

Most of the actors and actresses I've known have been pretty decent people. But when the ones who don't get parts very often are finally cast, they can become very demanding and equally ungracious. Must be all that pent-up anxiety. Jennifer is an exception. Nothing ruffles her and she is always very polite. But then, she works all the time.

The musicians I've known can get very nasty with each other, but have no reason to be rude to the people who work for them. The employees in the lower echelons of the music business have nothing but praise for the artists whom they serve. But I've seen actors — for no apparent reason — become imperious and condescending with "noncreative" theater personnel.

An example springs to mind. Picture me at the window of the box office. Phones were ringing and the callers were being put on hold. A line was forming that reached the curb. The wind was furious and the temperature, without mercy. Suddenly, Joe Actor cuts to the front of the line shouting,

"I'M AN ACTOR" to the insignificant non-actors who have been waiting, shivering in the cold.

"I need two seats for Saturday night and they have to be good."

"Saturday night is sold out."

"They're for my agent."

I'm not impressed. I wouldn't care if they were for Genghis Khan. "You should have ordered them earlier, we're sold out."

"I'm the star of the show."

I'm still not impressed. "Read my lips. We are sold out," I enunciate very carefully.

"I'll have your pecker on a platter if you don't give me two tickets for Saturday night."

"Sue me."

"I'll have you fired."

"Go ahead and try. You won't be the first."

"Why are you giving me such a hard time?"

My thoughts exactly. "I'm only doing the job they're paying me to do. I can't give you what I don't have."

"Can't you bump someone with a reservation?"

"No, I can't. *That* would be grounds for dismissal," I explained.

"What can I do?"

"Get your agent tickets for another performance. There are plenty of tickets for Friday night."

"She can't come on Friday night."

"Then I can't help you. Meanwhile, in case you hadn't noticed, there's a line of people waiting who were here before you."

He glanced around and scowled. "I don't give a shit, I need two tickets for Saturday night."

"The only thing I can do is notify you if we get a cancellation."

"What are the chances?"

"There's no way of predicting. Sometimes people cancel, usually they don't."

"What should I tell my agent?"

"Tell her you did your best."

He stomped away screaming something about how stupid box office treasurers are.

There was a cancellation the next day. Two seats in the last row. I figured I'd be a nice guy. I contacted the production manager and told him I was holding two Saturday night tickets for Joe Actor. He appeared at the window a few hours later.

"I heard you're holding two tickets for me, for Saturday night?"

"That's right. They're eighteen dollars each, that'll be thirty-six dollars please."

"I'm supposed to get comps."

"I checked out our records and you've already gotten your allotment of comps."

"Why are you giving me such a hard time?"

"I'm only doing my job, don't take it personally."

"No more comps?"

"That's what I said."

"All right, all right, I'll pay." He reached for his wallet. "Where are they?"

"Last row, two seats from the center aisle."

"Not good enough."

"It's all I've got."

Meanwhile, a line has formed behind him and the people — I mean non-actors — are standing in the cold, awaiting their turn.

"This theater sucks."

"That's one man's opinion."

"You suck."

"Just because you're an actor doesn't give you the right to be rude to me. Do you want these tickets or not? There are other customers waiting."

169

He scowled and said, "Okay, you win, I'll take 'em."

"Cash or charge?"

"Check."

"We don't accept checks."

He looked at me like he was going to explode. Shook his head as though I'd planned all of this just to torture him. He flung a credit card at me. I filled out the form. He signed it and I gave him the tickets.

"Fuck you!" he said.

"You're welcome," I said audibly. "Eat shit and die," I said silently.

That night I called and gave the boss my two week's notice. I was tired of the job, burned out actually. A person can stand only so much negativity. Machines would be perfect for box office work. You can scream at a computer for days, call it every obscene name you can think of, and it will never feel hurt or insulted.

Fortunately, my writing income was reaching the point where I would have been able to quit soon anyway. Mike helped out with short-term loans during the interim.

*

Without my knowing it, Donald had gathered together the sketches and writing that we had done based on each other's work. Multitextured pencil or charcoal drawings juxtaposed with poems or short prose vignettes. There was no central theme or concept, just a varied assemblage of words and images. He titled it *A Parcel Of Pieces* and sent a manuscript to a publisher who specialized in collaborations between artists and writers. I suddenly found myself to be coauthor of a soon-to-be-published book.

We agreed that it should bear a memorial dedication to Lorenzo.

When Donald received the letter of acceptance, he called to tell me the news. We decided to meet at the Corral to celebrate. Mike was busy with a production of *The Miser* by Moliere. Benjamin was in Chicago visiting his parents.

Donald and I stood toward the rear of the bar, near the jukebox. Stocked with classic Motown, the latest British synth-pop, a few easy listening standards, some dance numbers, and a smattering of country tunes.

I gazed at the familiar interior. A small, womb-like structure, the Corral's walls sported cowboy regalia — boots, bridles, and saddles — and a huge wagon wheel studded with flashing red lights was suspended from the ceiling.

Donald played the jukebox and bought us drinks. "Congratulations," he said. "You're about to graduate from writer to author."

"What's the difference?"

"Writer's write stories and articles. Authors write books."

"But I didn't really write a book," I protested. "Jotting down a few poems and sketches is nothing like writing a novel. I don't *feel* like I've written a book."

"Be that as it may, you're about to become the author of a book."

"Coauthor."

Just then a sculpted, bronzed stud entered the Corral and sauntered to the bar.

"Not bad," said Donald.

"You're married," I reminded him.

"I can still look," he said.

"Yes, but you can't touch."

"I'm not fooling around with anyone besides Benjamin until they find a cure."

"Same here."

"I hope it's soon."

"Me too," I said. "Not that I want to fool around. I'm very happy with Mike. But not wanting to and not being able to are different things."

"Yeah. We at least deserve the choice."

"AIDS makes it easier to be faithful," I said, finishing my tequila and grapefruit juice.

"But being faithful isn't in everyone's nature."

"I wonder what'll happen when the epidemic is over?"

"That's easy," said Donald, flourishing his hand like a magician. "Some people will fuck and suck like there's no tomorrow. Others will probably be cautious for the rest of their lives."

"What about the younger generations of gay guys who haven't matured yet," I said, "I wonder how they'll react."

"Things will most likely go back to the way they were. But now people know about safe sex. That ought to alter a few things in the future."

"Like the VD rate," I said.

"Here's to no more VD," said Donald. We clinked our glasses and left a short while later.

We wound up dancing until after four in the morning.

*

Summer again. I'm sitting by the window in a tanktop and briefs, perspiring like a fountain. Sometimes I go to a movie just for the two hours of air-conditioning. Even though the sight below is far more aesthetically pleasing than any movie could ever be. How could anything compete with the arms and shoulders of the man about to cross the intersection? What would I rather look at than the powerful thighs spread before me on the bench in the park?

It's difficult to disguise anything in summer clothing. So, along with the attractive flesh, you also see a lot of bodies that go unattended. Flabby or skinny. Nothing to excite one sexually. I'm sure they have lovely personalities.

Too hot for anything physical, I simply gaze and devour with my eyes. And sometimes get lost in rambling thoughts. Or measure progress. Or plot future strategies.

One thing I have learned about life is that it resembles the art of mountain climbing. It is a form of discipline. There are rules and regulations that depend on the natural order.

You can't, for example, just switch mountains in midair. You must crawl down the side of the one you've deemed un-

172

conquerable. Then find a proper starting point to again com-
mence the upward struggle. And it's not until you've passed
the equivalent point — where you abandoned your previous
ascent — on the new mountain, that you can claim any credit.
Acknowledging the earlier defeat in addition to having to wait
so long for a little something to be proud of is exhausting,
frustrating, demeaning.

Still, if you are able to learn anything at all from prior
experience, the next mountain might not be quite as tough.
The last one, if you were paying any attention, should have
taught you a few shortcuts, a couple of lessons. And perhaps
it even whispered a few secrets that you jotted down so you
wouldn't forget.

*

Last weekend, for the first time, Mike and I had Magda
all to ourselves. She'd spent an occasional night with us, but
this was our first weekend. Jennifer and Russell were going
to Atlantic City and dropped Magda by on Friday afternoon.

Mike was sitting crosslegged on the couch, working on
some set designs for a new play and I was typing by the
window. The buzzer rang and Mike opened the door.

Jennifer ooed and ahed over Mike's sketches. Russell sat
on the couch and thumbed through a copy of *Beefcake*. He
glanced at a picture of two naked men lying in a hayloft. His
eyes opened wide when he turned the page. He gulped and
closed the magazine. Magda, wearing a red T-shirt that said
"Youngster," was looking at the page I was typing.

"Don't bother him," said Russell, "let him work."

"It's all right," I said, "I'm used to typing with her
around."

"What are you working on?" asked Jennifer, pulling her
hair from her shoulders and flinging it back.

"A novel."

"Oh, really?" Russell said. "What's it about, mate?"

"A lot of different things," Mike interjected. "We're all

in it, in fact. Some of it's funny, some sad. And there're aliens in it too. Weird."

"Aliens," said Russell, "sounds cheeky."

"So, what's planned for the weekend?" Jennifer inquired.

I turned away from the typewriter. "I'm cooking dinner tonight. Nothing fancy. Pasta and asparagus. Ice cream after."

"Oh, good," said Magda, surveying the video tapes.

"Tomorrow we're seeing a new play produced by the Harlem Children's Theater. Sunday afternoon we're picnicking in Central Park and that night we're going to see *Fantasia*," I said.

Magda pulled a cassette from the shelf and gave it to Mike. "Can we watch this?"

"Of course," said Mike.

"I didn't know you guys had a VCR," said Russell.

"Mike bought it for Hanukkah," I explained.

"What cassette is that?" asked Jennifer.

"*Romeo and Juliet*, the MacMillan ballet based on Prokofiev," said Mike. "It's Magda's favorite."

Russell picked her up and placed her on his knee. "I didn't know you wanted to be a dancer," he said.

"I don't want to be a dancer," she countered.

"Oh," said Jennifer, "you want to be a choreographer?"

Magda shook her head. "No."

Mike kneeled before her, swept some ringlets from her forehead and said, "Tell Mommy and Russell what you want to be when you grow up."

"A producer," she said.

Jennifer chuckled. "Who told you to say that?"

"No one."

Jennifer looked at me. "Did you tell her to say that?"

"No."

"Mike?"

"Not me," he said. "That's what she told me a few weeks ago when I asked her."

Jennifer turned to Russell. "You?"

"No, ducky."

She looked down at Magda. "You thought of that all by yourself?"

"Yes, Mommy."

"That's wonderful," she said, gathering her daughter in her arms.

"You know," Russell chuckled, then looked at Mike, "all this time I thought you and Magda were watching a lot of *television*."

"Videos," said Mike, grinning. "Mostly old movies, but sometimes an opera or ballet."

Jennifer pretended she was slapping herself on her face. "So that's what she meant when she said you guys have a better TV than us."

"I guess it's time we got a VCR," said Russell. He stood up and moved toward the door. "We should get on, love."

"Have a nice weekend," I said.

"Bye," said Magda.

"So long," said Mike.

"Take care, gents," said Russell.

"Don't do anything we wouldn't do," Jennifer smirked.

"We won't," Magda assured her.

I locked the door behind them. Mike placed Magda on his lap and tickled her chin. When *Romeo and Juliet* was over, I started preparing dinner.

It turned out to be a lovely weekend.

A few days later I was standing on line at the supermarket, my cart almost overflowing. On the magazine stand was a row of weekly tabloids. One headline screamed "UFO LANDS IN CENTRAL PARK!"

Since reading those words I've been on the lookout for Aliens. But I haven't run into any yet. That I know of. So far. Of course, they could have wound up on the Upper East Side. And I can't imagine what might happen to them there.

BOOKS FROM BANNED BOOKS

A Herd of Tiny Elephants,
  Stan Leventhal $8.95
Mountain Climbing in Sheridan Square,
  Stan Leventhal $8.95
Common Sons,
  Ronald Donaghe $8.95
Sacred Cows,
  Jed A. Bryan $8.95
A Cry in the Desert,
  Jed A. Bryan $9.95
Two Novellas, After All This and Walking Water,
  Thom Nickels $8.95
Fine Lines,
  Gerard Curry $7.95
Tangled Sheets,
  Gerard Curry $7.95
Like Coming Home: Coming-Out Letters (Nonfiction),
  Edited by Meg Umans $7.95
Dairy of a New York Queen,
  William Barber $8.95
gay(s)language,
  H. Max $4.95
Kite Music,
  Gary Shellhart $8.95
Days in the Sun,
  Drew Kent $8.95
Fairy Tales Mother Never Told You,
  Benjamin Eakin $5.95
The Gay of Cooking Cookbook,
  The Kitchen Fairy (distributed for Fairy Publications) $10.95

These books are available from your favorite bookstore or by mail from:

BANNED BOOKS
Number 292, P.O. Box 33280, Austin, Texas 78764

Add 10% of order total (minimum $1.50, maximum $3.00) for postage and handling. Texas residents, please also add 8% sales tax. Send your name and address for our free current catalog and to be added to our confidential mailing list.